# Season of the Rainbirds

# NADEEM ASLAM

ff

FABER & FABER

First published in 1993 by
Andre Deutsch Limited

This paperback edition
first published in 2005 by
Faber & Faber Limited
Bloomsbury House
74–77 Great Russell Street
London WC1B 3DA

This paperback edition published in 2015

Printed and bound by CPI Group (UK) Ltd, Croydon, CR0 4YY

A CIP record for this book
is available from the British Library

ISBN 978–0–571–31330–3

2 4 6 8 10 9 7 5 3 1

For Naeema

# NOTE

All characters in this novel are fictional; most of the events are, too. However:

– the terrorist attack mentioned in 'Wednesday' (chapter 7) is based on the first attempt on General Zia's life: on 7 February 1982, the Al-Zulifiquar (the terrorist team led by Benazir Bhutto's brother, Murtaza) fired a SAM-7 missile at a plane carrying the General.

– The *Little Green Book* containing the 'President's thoughts', mentioned in 'Thursday' (chapter 8), did exist; it was commissioned by Ayub Khan during his rule (1958–69).

*

The quotations from the Qur'an in this book are from N.J. Dawood's translation for the Penguin Classics series.

I am indebted to Tariq Ali for his excellent books on Pakistan, *Pakistan: Military Rule or People's Power?* (Cape, 1970) and *Can Pakistan Survive?* (Penguin Books, 1983); the books provided social and political context for some of my childhood memories.

A glossary of Urdu words used in the novel will be found at the end of this book.

N.A.

# PRINCIPAL CHARACTERS

| | |
|---|---|
| MAULANA HAFEEZ | Aged cleric of one of the two mosques in the town. |
| MAULANA DAWOOD | Cleric of the other mosque. |
| JUDGE ANWAR | Powerful local figure. |
| ASGRI ANWAR | Judge Anwar's wife and mother of his seven daughters. |
| AZHAR | Deputy Commissioner. |
| ELIZABETH MASSIH | Azhar's Christian mistress. |
| BENJAMIN MASSIH | Roadsweeper. Elizabeth's father. |
| MUJEEB ALI | Local landowner. |
| NABILA ALI | Mujeeb Ali's wife and mother of his five daughters. |
| ARSHAD ALI | Mujeeb Ali's youngest brother. |
| KALSUM | Widow receiving pension from Mujeeb Ali for death of son in political rally. |
| SURAYA | Kalsum's sister on visit from Canada seeking divorce from husband Burkat. |
| YUSUF RAO | Lawyer and former political activist. Old university friend of Mr Kasmi. |
| MR KASMI | Retired schoolmaster. |
| ZÉBUN | Ex-courtesan. Mr Kasmi's landlady. |
| ALICE | Zébun's Christian servant girl. |
| ZAFRI | The butcher. Friend and confidant of Nabi, the barber. |

| | |
|---|---|
| MANSOOR | Close neighbour of Maulana Hafeez. |
| GUL-KALAM | Nightwatchman. |
| SAIF AZIZ | 'Metropolitan' journalist and ex-political activist. |

If I'd been told as a child what the life of an adult is like, I wouldn't have believed it. I'd never have believed it could be so unfinished.

John Berger, *Once in Europa*

———

*Fish.*

*The cook lifts the damp dark-red cloth to reveal a row of quicksilver fish, overlapping each other like fallen dominoes. Wherever we are, whatever we're doing, we leave the blinding white light of the summer day for the gloom of the kitchen. The rumpled cloth has fallen to the floor. We hold our breaths as the cook picks up the serrated knife – the knife we are forbidden to sharpen pencils with. Could this be it? Our chins tickle as the tip of the knife is inserted below a fish's mouth. Then the cook makes a rapid stem-to-stern tear and splits open our stomachs, pushes in two large fingers to uproot our guts and, without looking, hurls them into the bowl set beside her on the table. Still dizzy from the sunlight, we dip tentative fingers into the grisly mess and feel for shahzadi Mahar-un-Nisa's diamond ring. No, this was not the fish that swallowed it. We wait for the next fish to be opened. Our fingertips are coated with pink tissue fluid.*

*But the cook asks us to leave; the knife is raised in the air – a gesture reminiscent of early April when we enter the kitchen to steal aambis. Then, a ladle – a triangular plume of sweetly scented vapour attached to it – might be raised in the air. The cook bears provocation patiently but doesn't like us inside the kitchen. She doesn't flinch from tasting half-cooked dishes to check if the salt was remembered. If she thinks something is worthless she calls it 'the ash of seven ovens'. Not only is it worthless, there is also so much of it! We time our raids well: we sneak in when water is being added to the chaval. A specific number of glassfuls has to be added and the cook cannot turn around without breaking her concentration. She is tense as she counts: '. . . three . . . four, get away from there, five . . . six . . . you'll make me, seven . . . lose track, eight . . . eight, eight . . . nine.' Once free, she comes to the door and shouts across the courtyard, 'You'll all die of yarkan and I'll get the blame. No more aambis.'*

1

*Men with black beards are to be avoided; while those with white beards are kind and gentle. We hide under the bed and, through the serpentine curves of the bobin lace, listen to Mother and Uncle Shujahat talk to each other in raised voices. Uncle Shujahat has a black beard; it reaches down to his navel. Mother says, 'You're using religion as an excuse to withdraw from the world. You're running away from your responsibilities.' Uncle Shujahat says, 'We were not brought up to talk about God-prophet in this manner. If only Father-ji could hear you.' Mother shouts back, 'Father-ji was religious but he kept things in proportion. He even sent me, a girl, to Lahore to get a university degree. He didn't mind my living away from home. And that was twenty years ago.'*

*Uncle Shujahat doesn't like toys. He takes our dolls and masks from us, breaks them in two, and then hands them back. He says images of God's creations are not allowed in the house, not while he's visiting.*

*The servants arrive for work in the middle of the morning. The homes where children don't have to be sent to school – and, therefore, the day's chores can begin immediately – are dealt with by them before our house. The first sounds of the day have vanished by this time: the bell of the candy-floss maker, Bibi-ji, reciting the Qur'an on the veranda, the 'aa . . . aa . . . come . . . come' of the dove-fancier who waves a bamboo pole, with its red ribbon, at his doves. Bibi-ji has long since harvested today's motya blossoms – before the rising sun could take away the fragrance – and fastened them into a garland for her hair.*

*With a pack-animal-like stampede, the servants begin their work; putting us to flight with the merciless swish of the linen, the beating of the rugs, the arcs from the hose-pipes above our heads, the spreading – like a flapping of wings – of the mats for preparing vegetables, the stubborn dusting and the obstinate sweeping. The air becomes charged with violence. The legs of the rope cots are taken out of the bowls of water – dead insects float on the surface of the stale water – and the milky fishbones are collected from the rims of last night's dinner plates.*

*During the afternoon hours the women sit on the cool screened veranda and talk amongst themselves. A young mother asks what the scarlet pimples on the newborn's upper arms could be. Smallpox, replies the eldest, and advises that the child be put in quarantine. The cook explains how to catch out a vendor who is trying to pass off tortoise's eggs as hen's. Someone else instructs that vegetables that grow beneath the surface of the earth should be cooked with the lid on; and those that grow above, with the lid off. While they sit on the darkened veranda, we swim about in the sunlight of the courtyard, burning with magnifying glasses the insects that have been sucked into the pedestal fan. Occasionally, we have to stop and look up: the adults are referring to our world: which one of us had smiled at nine weeks old, under which bush a dead yellow-striped snake was found one winter, the story of a schoolboy who got left behind, locked in, in his school over the summer holidays; how he ate chalk and paper and left tearful messages on the blackboard; and what happened when his body was discovered in September. We move closer to the veranda, pretending all the while to be interested only in our games – busy examining the pieces of coral trapped inside the marbles, waiting for the rosebuds inside the old necklace beads to open, discussing the inverted tears floating in the paperweights stolen from the study to add to our collection of glass spheres.*

*With the first call for the afternoon prayers this lazy calm comes to an end. The house is plunged once again into energetic activity. With an 'up, O mortal' each, the women pull themselves upright and disappear into the rooms. It's time for us to walk the two blocks to the mosque for our Qur'anic lessons. Beads and sticks and dolls are taken from our hands and we are coaxed into remembering where we left our scarves yesterday.*

*The street is still shut when we step into the molten-gold atmosphere of mid-afternoon. The houses face each other across the passages like armies on an ancient Arabian battlefield. The hot air carries the noise of inaudible rattles. We narrow our eyes against the glare. Beating their wings, the birds too are leaving the trees for the mosque. The leaves hang like limp hands from the branches. We try to think of the cool blue river and, turning around, glance towards where the river wets the horizon. But the river, too, seems helpless before the insanity of the sun, lying like an exhausted lizard at the end of the street.*

*We walk past the house with the blue door. It has been made clear to us that we are to walk quietly by this house, never accept an invitation to step inside, never return the smile of the woman of the house, nor glance at the old man who sometimes looks out of the upstairs window; at our peril are we to be tempted by the flowers lying under the eaves, or by the figs that the storms shake loose. But our shadows dare each other. One of them is foolish enough to climb on to the doorstep but is pulled away just before it can reach the door bell.*

*And what might the penalty be for disobedience? We round the corner and fear all but suffocates us, an intense streak of fear that is not easy to extirpate. Recumbent under the arch of a portico the blind woman takes her siesta. Wrinkles gouge her face and rags of every colour are wrapped around her body. Her eyes, though bereft of vision, radiate a feral inhumanity. A gnarled right hand, palm upward, lies on the cement floor, while the other rests – permanently, we believe – on the shoulder of a little girl. The girl's thicket-like hair stirs and her eyes watch us vacantly when we enter her field of vision. Set alongside the air of limitless danger that attends the old woman, the girl appears helpless – as helpless as the sparrow's bote that fell out of its nest last spring. All day long the girl guides the old woman through the streets, begging. We drag our inquisitive shadows towards the mosque, eyes downturned. A kite wails overhead.*

*The dangers of the street are counterpointed by the calm firefly-like presence of the cleric's wife. Her smile casts a delicate spell. She sits before us and we recite for her from our Qur'anic readers. Each reader is one-thirtieth of the Qur'an. The language is alien to us – we have not been taught the alphabet – but we have learned the shapes of the words by heart. The cleric's wife gives our old readers new shiny greeting-card bindings. We wait by her side as she stitches a tattered reader inside a camel-and-bedouin-beneath-a-crescent Eid greeting, or inside a pair-of-doves wedding invitation. Sometimes she polishes her wedding ring with ground turmeric.*

*On the wall behind her is a calendar which shows the whole of Ramadan in red and both the Eids in gold. Next to the calendar is the pendulum clock; it is as ornate as a woman's brooch. We wish for six o'clock never to arrive, for it never to be time for us to leave here.*

*Perhaps if we pray hard enough . . .*

*The clock strikes six, the hands divide the clock's face into two half-moons. The cleric's wife offers us one last exultant and forgiving smile. We kiss our readers and slip them into satin envelopes. Our shoes are set in rows at the edge of the vestibule, like boats at a Bengali ghat. The streets are full of inky shadows. But before we leave there is a quarrel. A combed-out flourish of the cleric's wife's hair has been found on the floor and we have to settle who gets to keep it between the pages of their reader.*

*Wednesday*

—

Every day during the last hour before sunrise Maulana Hafeez went into the mosque to say the optional pre-dawn prayers. In the isolation and deep silence of the mosque he abased himself before God – bent his body at the waist, straightened and bowed. Afterwards, as sunrise and the time to make the call for the first obligatory prayers of the day approached, he rolled out the ranks of mats that stood leaning against the walls and, working methodically down the length of the hall, placed a straw skullcap and a rosary at the head of each mat. Not many men came to the mosque at dawn but Maulana Hafeez always spread out every mat, covering the entire floor of the hall, setting each place with meticulous care. At around eight o'clock, when the shops along the side of the mosque building were being opened and school-boys in slate-grey uniform hurried down the narrow street, he returned home to breakfast and slept until noon.

Through the half-open door of his bedroom Maulana Hafeez could see into the kitchen across the courtyard. His wife – obscured by the drizzle, faint as a watermark – was preparing breakfast. The house was connected to the mosque by a veranda and the two buildings shared a courtyard enclosed by some of the trees mentioned in the Qur'an – pomegranates and figs and the larger, more tree-like, olives. Maulana Hafeez rose from the chair where he had dozed since his return from the mosque. It was a dull windless morning, clouds brushed low over the roof of the house. Maulana Hafeez knew that today he would have to forgo his after-breakfast sleep: there had been a death in town. Outside in the street a motor sounded – rising to a maximum and receding – accompanied by the noise of splashing water. The rains had broken at last. Maulana Hafeez draped a towel over his head and began carrying the flowerpots that edged the veranda to the centre of the courtyard.

The day's rain would revive the tired foliage. After the flowerpots Maulana Hafeez took down the ferns hanging from the eaves and placed them in a cluster around the other pots.

When he came in out of the drizzle his wife poured him a cup of tea – the second of many that Maulana Hafeez would drink during the course of the day. Maulana Hafeez dried his face and beard with the towel and took the cup.

'You were in Raiwind during the month of that train crash, Maulana-ji,' the woman said; she was thinking about the lost mail-bags. She was fair-skinned, frail, and her abundant hair was as white as the stole covering her head.

The cleric made an effort to remember. On his forehead there was a small bruise, the size of a teddy-paisa coin, proclaiming the zeal of his obeisance in prayer.

'Nineteen years,' the woman said and rose to her feet. From outside she brought into the kitchen two chairs and set them with their backs to the fire. Over the chairs she spread the clothes Maulana Hafeez was to wear to Judge Anwar's funeral.

'I heard a papiha singing somewhere,' she said. 'It must be monsoon.'

Maulana Hafeez nodded. 'It's been singing since dawn.'

Resin sizzled, hissing angrily on the surface of the blazing wood; the fire burned, the flames horizontal against the base of the pan in which something fragrant simmered. Maulana Hafeez looked up at his wife and said, 'I *do* remember something about an infant surviving a train crash.' He searched his wife's face for confirmation. 'Was that the same accident?'

'You're right, Maulana-ji,' she said. 'Strange that you should remember that. A little boy *was* found under the wreckage, five days later. There was a picture of him in the newspaper.' Like everyone else in town Maulana Hafeez's wife addressed him as 'Maulana-ji'; she had never used the familiar 'tu'.

'God is merciful,' Maulana Hafeez said quietly; other details of the disaster were coming back to him.

His wife came back to the stool and, removing the pan from the fire, got ready to bake chappatis. She tested the temperature of the

10

baking-iron with a pinch of flour – it turned brown immediately, the smell of singed starch spreading through the small room. She pulled out the wood to moderate the heat and, with rapid clapping gestures, began to flatten a ball of dough between her palms. Blue veins were visible beneath the skin of her knuckles. Maulana Hafeez looked out at the silent mosque – it looked like a collection of glittering vases floating in the drizzle.

'I still haven't announced the death on the loudspeaker,' he said.

His wife shook her head. 'There's no need, Maulana-ji,' she said, carefully spreading the flat circle of dough on the baking-iron. 'I'm sure the whole town has known about it since four o'clock.'

Behind the mosque, in that part of town which was once a Hindu neighbourhood, most of the doors on to the streets were open. Women stood on doorsteps, arranging their pale mourning shawls over their heads, hesitating before stepping into the drizzle. A crowd, mostly men, swarmed outside Judge Anwar's house; and everyone, even those standing still, appeared purposeful. The only women were a few beggars, and there were some children, again mostly boys. A servant girl, carrying a bucket of water and a twig-broom, came out of the house. Judge Anwar had suffered from diabetes most of his adult life. Some hours before his death – before the break-in – he had got out of bed and squatted to urinate by the bedroom door that gave on to the portico. The urine had dried on the floor – a dark line on the grey cement – and tiny brown ants were chipping off the flaky crystals of sugar. The girl began to wash the floor, drowning and sweeping away the ants with her broom. Beyond the far end of the street was the empty plain where a Hindu temple had stood at other times. After the Partition, Hindus had emigrated to India and Muslims coming in the other direction to replace them – to settle in the new homeland – had torn down many of the sacred places of their predecessors. A large section of the temple had had to be dynamited. The conical tower was reduced to rubble in seconds, the large bronze bell tolling as it fell to jubilant applause from the onlookers.

Beyond the empty lot was the river, appearing like a silver thread except where obscured by the wild summer grasses that grew between the still-remaining parts of the temple floor. The smell of water – sluggish and uncomfortable – was in the air, eddying down the street. Azhar drew breath sharply as he entered the muddy street. A very fine drizzle was falling, its impact barely registering on the surface of the puddles; palls of dark cloud surrounded the sun. A small boy ran out of a house and headed, in front of Azhar, towards the judge's house. From inside the boy's home a woman's coarse voice shouted reproaches and threatened punishments; but the boy was out of earshot.

Azhar arrived at Judge Anwar's house. The talk became muffled and the crowd made way for him to reach the front door. Someone who was smoking a cigarette, and who exhaled smoke from his lungs fast as Azhar approached, reached out his hand and said, 'They left without managing to take anything.' Azhar nodded without shifting his gaze, nor did he alter his precise pace.

The house was full of people, and here, too, everyone seemed in the middle of performing some important task. Two men had been to the mosque and borrowed the low wooden platform on which corpses were washed. All the rooms opening on to the courtyard were being prepared to receive mourners. Most of the furniture had been removed from these rooms – only the heavy beds remained, standing on their sides against the walls – and the familiar rooms appeared, Azhar noted, at once spacious and alien. White sheets covered the floors. Photographs and portraits had either been removed to other rooms or turned face to the walls. However, the framed reminders of the dead man's career had been left untouched: still crowding the shelves and mantelpieces were addresses, tributes and sapas-namas, each with the text printed elegantly between garlanded borders on shiny paper. Someone on his way out of a room stopped on seeing Azhar and said, 'The shotgun was a Lee-Enfield.'

Azhar stood outside the room and softly cleared his throat before entering. The lowing of the heavy door caused many women inside to look up. They sat on sheets spread over the floor; it was possible to tell from the faces distorted by interrupted sleep which of them had been in the house since dawn. They covered their heads as Azhar entered.

The body was laid out on a cot in the centre of the room. A length of white cloth covered it; part of one heel had remained exposed and its tough cracked skin seemed to impart a pink hue to the edges of the sheet. Flanked on either side by her two eldest daughters Asgri Anwar sat cross-legged at the head of the cot. Azhar uncovered Judge Anwar's face. The fabric resisted separation at the wound – the shot had obliterated the throat.

Dr Sharif entered the room. He had been sent for because one of the daughters had fainted earlier in the morning. As he advanced, the physician had to bend down several times and ask to be allowed through. The women shifted grudgingly. Because he insisted once a year on immunising children against cholera and typhoid the physician was barred from many homes. Many mothers did not want the limbs of their children 'turned into sieves'. Undeterred, Dr Sharif would drag inside any child that passed by the surgery and, pinning the kicking and screaming girl or boy to the floor with his knee, inject the dose.

'I sleep in the next room,' Asgri was telling Azhar. 'I heard nothing but the shot.'

Azhar looked about him uncomfortably. There was no air in the room. 'We'll get them, apa,' he said quietly. 'Whoever they were.'

Asgri lowered her head and made a dismissive wave with her hand. Suddenly one of the girls let out a scream and began hitting her head against the leg of the cot. At the same time she beat her breast with both hands. Her mother and sister and some of the other women tried to restrain her; the corpse shook gently on the cot. Judge Anwar was a large man, who had had the bearing of a Sikh. But the fierce constitution of his younger days had suffered in recent years from diabetes. The condition became more besetting when, on learning that the imported insulin he injected into his veins daily was extracted from the pancreas of pigs, he stopped the injections, turning instead to a local remedy – drinking boiled loquat leaves.

Dr Sharif approached. 'I've given her something,' he said to Asgri. 'She'll sleep for a few hours.' Then he turned to speak to Azhar but his words were completely drowned out: two men had come in to collect the body for washing and the women had begun their wailing. The youngest daughter – a girl as beautiful as a seventh consecutive daughter had to be – slept peacefully in the arms of an elderly neighbour. One of the men carefully lifted the sheet off the corpse's face to allow Asgri to see her husband for the last time. During the washing rituals the body was said to sever all ties made on earth; afterwards, therefore, a woman could not look at the man who had married her, it being a sin to lay eyes on a stranger.

'Has Maulana Hafeez arrived yet?' Asgri asked.

The man shook his head.

'I want Maulana Hafeez to supervise everything,' Asgri said curtly. 'Everything is to be done according to the Sunnat.' She nodded towards the man's hands.

The man's fingers let drop the corner of the sheet. 'Everything will be done according to the strictures of the Sunnat.'

'I hear you've added neem leaves to the water,' Asgri said; and turning to the woman sitting beside her she said, 'Is that allowed?'

Dr Sharif half-knelt towards the window and said above the din, 'Neem leaves serve as disinfectant. It's advisable to add a few to the water. It's common practice.'

Asgri gripped the edge of the cot firmly. 'Call Maulana Hafeez.' And, as though responding to the call, the loudspeaker mounted on the mosque's minaret came on with a hoarse growl and Maulana Hafeez proceeded to announce the death and the time set for the funeral prayers.

People in the street listened intently to the announcement. Each relayed word carried a tiny echo which in turn was accompanied

14

by another echo, fainter still. The whole effect was that of a reflection on gently disturbed water. A sewer-worker, a Christian, went along the street, dragging behind him the long flexible bamboo pole used for unblocking the underground sewage channels. As he turned the corner the trailing end of the pole – more than fifteen yards separated the two ends – shot across the width of the street. The police inspector, a short man with a round stomach and a balding head, managed to step out of the way just in time to avoid a blow on the ankles. 'Christian bastard,' he murmured, shaking his head. Azhar was coming out on to the courtyard when the inspector entered the house.

'The chief inspector, the superintendent of police and the chief superintendent have been informed,' the inspector told Azhar. Azhar nodded. Elsewhere, as deputy commissioner, Azhar's rank would have been too high for him to involve himself in such matters. As it was, he lived in the town – two streets away from Judge Anwar's house – and the dead man had also been a friend.

Together the two men walked through the labyrinthine house room by room – each one high-ceilinged and excessively decorated – and tried to work out a possible sequence of events following the break-in, Azhar listening patiently to the theories that the inspector had had time to formulate since dawn. They asked the servants to open up the locked rooms. They peered under the beds and behind the cupboards and armoires. They unbolted several windows, all of them set in deep recesses and many of them never opened by the family, and looked out – without consequence – on to the back lane. They stood on the elaborate balconies that kept the edges of the street in shade at midday, and considered the drop on to the street below. 'One of them probably climbed on to the roof' – the police inspector pointed at the displaced cover of the water-tank at the top of the staircase – 'and came down to let the others in.'

'The servants will have to be questioned,' Azhar said.

Outside in the street Gul-kalam, the nightwatchman, was talking excitedly to a group assembled around him. He moved his shoulders and hands boisterously. On seeing Azhar and the police inspector appear at the front door he became suddenly grim and, abandoning his audience, crossed the street hurriedly.

'I was two streets away when I heard the shot,' he said in his clipped north-western accent. 'I couldn't have done anything.' He had pale blue eyes which he kept rimmed with antimony; his great bushy moustache curved into his mouth, obscuring the upper lip.

'You've already made your statement, Gul-kalam.' Azhar placed his hand on the man's shoulder.

But Gul-kalam shook his head miserably. 'I'm worthless. I couldn't save him.'

'Later, Gul-kalam,' the police inspector said impatiently. 'First, get these people to clear the street.' And turning to Azhar he said, 'We had better erect a shamiana out here. Soon there won't be enough room inside.'

Gul-kalam had walked away from them. The brass whistle, which he would blow at the ends of each street on his rounds, dangled from his neck. On his feet he wore brown leather sandals whose thick soles held his feet inches above the mud. They watched him in silence for a few moments.

'So,' the inspector turned to Azhar and said, through a half-smile, 'what's this I hear about *you*, deputy-sahib?'

Azhar looked at him in incomprehension. A man carrying on his head an enormous basket as wide and flat as a stork's nest, heaped with flowers, sidled past him and went into the house. 'What?' said Azhar, at the same time expelling the heavy fragrance of marigolds from his lungs.

The inspector smiled more openly. 'The men who went to your house this morning to tell you about the death say there was a woman there with you.'

Through the small window of his room the old man saw Kalsum and Suraya open and enter the cemetery gate. He stopped kneading his limp biceps and went to that corner of the room where, in

16

the angle between two walls, there was a heap of soil covered with a tough canvas sheet. With slow shovelfuls he filled a large basket and, heaving it up to his left shoulder, followed the two women down the narrow path of cracked slabs.

Kalsum squatted by her son's grave; in lowering herself she drew the tails of her loose tunic between the back of her thighs and her calves, to prevent the hemline from getting muddied. One by one she picked up the rotting leaves that had accumulated around the grave since her last visit. Suraya walked around and began to clear the other side of the mound. The drizzle had ceased, and on the trunks and boughs of the large trees growing amongst the graves, mottled patterns left by last year's honey-fungus showed vivid, lit by the raking afternoon light. A few of the graves had planted at their heads the colours – small square or triangular flags – of the fakirs and sufis that the dead person had followed in life. The wet rags hung stiffly, clinging to the poles, the surface-tension of water holding the folds firmly in place.

'You should have waited for a dry day,' the old man said to Kalsum. With a heavy sigh he brought down the basket of soil and remained bent at the waist – hands gripping the rim of the basket – for a few moments, trying to catch his breath.

Kalsum did not look up; she simply said, 'I come on the last Wednesday of every month, baba. Have you forgotten?' Suraya had cleared her side of the grave and was standing up, cleaning her fingers with a handkerchief. The keeper's milky eyes examined her. She wore a large coat tightly fastened at the waist. The rigid fabric and exaggerated collar and cuffs gave it the appearance of a garment intended for a marionette, a doll.

'This is my sister, baba,' Kalsum said, 'Burkat's wife. Do you remember Burkat, baba?'

'Burkat,' the old man mumbled to himself, very quietly, as though turning in his mouth a piece of food never before tasted, waiting for it to release a flavour that the tongue might recognise. 'Little Kazo Nur's brother?'

Suraya nodded.

'Well, well,' he brightened. 'We are practically family then.' He laughed quietly to himself, pleased. The dark flesh on his cheeks had slackened with age and sunk into deep hollows on either side of the nose. 'But didn't he go to live in England?'

'Canada,' Kalsum said. 'They went to England first, but then they moved to Canada.'

'Canada,' he said lifting his head towards Suraya. 'Is that far from England?' And, narrowing his eyes to think, he added, 'Here to Karachi?'

'Much farther.'

Kalsum was spreading the soil evenly over the grave. The soil caught beneath her fingernails appeared green. Suraya too sat down once more and began to take handfuls from the basket. The old man pulled up a grass stem and, snapping it in two, began to pick his teeth. 'When did you come back?' he asked. 'From Canada.'

'Ten days.' Suraya packed the spongy soil tightly, pressing down with the palms of both her hands. The old man nodded and spat loudly over his shoulder. Sensing that he was about to speak again Kalsum chided gently, 'Baba, have you eaten crows? You are talking too much.'

At the other end of the graveyard a group of women emerged from the small enclosure, sheltered by a corrugated-iron roof, where funeral prayers were said. The iron rails of the enclosure were wrapped in trumpet bindweed. The keeper followed the sisters' glances and said, 'They are servants from Judge Anwar's house. The widow sent them to clean the floor of the jinaza-gah. I told them it is clean, it is swept every other day, but they wouldn't listen.'

A whole layer of soil was added to the mound and doused with the watering-can that the keeper fetched – spilling and splashing to his right and left – from the tap outside his room. Kalsum stood up. 'He would have been twenty-one this December.' She looked around and took in all the other graves.

The old man nodded slowly and looking at Suraya said, 'He was born three months before *my* boy.'

'He was a good son,' Kalsum said; she rubbed the palms of her hands hard against each other and the damp soil came off in thin, slender sickles and the skin beneath showed white.

'Mine would ruin me,' the keeper turned towards Kalsum and said. 'He's been nothing but trouble since he grew up. When he was a boy, people sent him on errands and gave him money afterwards. I would protest. Send him to do work, by all means, I said, it's good for a child to be obedient. But don't give him any money. A child shouldn't have money, he'll develop bad habits.'

Kalsum agreed and touched the old man's forearm. 'May God guide them, baba.'

'Now the shopkeepers are his friends. He gets them to write fake receipts and keeps the difference,' the keeper went on. 'He thinks I don't know, but I know.'

'He sent his mother to her grave,' Kalsum turned to her sister and said quietly; and to the keeper: 'Where is he now?'

'I've sent him to the fertiliser factory to buy a sack of lime. There wasn't going to be enough for the judge's grave.' As he spoke, the old man's adam's apple bobbed up and down. He placed the empty watering-can inside the basket and picked up the basket. 'Still,' he smiled, 'I could be rich soon. Perhaps I'll get a letter saying that nineteen years ago I had won a lottery.'

Suraya and Kalsum were walking down the path. Kalsum turned around. 'What are you talking about, baba?'

The keeper approached; he looked at her incredulously. 'You haven't heard about the letters?'

Kalsum shook her head. 'What letters?' Suraya had walked down to the tip of the path and, folding back the sleeves of her coat, was washing her hands at the tap.

'They've just found three sacks of letters that went missing after a train crash nineteen years ago,' the old man explained. 'The ones belonging to the two neighbouring towns have been delivered. It's our turn soon.'

Maulana Hafeez did not go home directly after the burial. First, aware that there would be a shortage of rosaries for the mourners, he instructed some of the younger men at the cemetery to carry the sacks of date pits, collected and stored for just such occasions, from the mosque to the judge's house. Then he walked to the lower part of the town. He went down the narrow, twisting alleyways, saying his rosary – the beads rising slowly towards his fingers and dropping one by one over the other side. It was the hottest hour of the day; the houses were shut and, apart from some schoolboys playing truant, the streets were deserted. Maulana Hafeez knocked on the door of a small adobe house. He informed the woman who came to the door, her clothes in disarray and her hair dishevelled – she had been taking her siesta – that her mother's grave was showing signs of neglect, it needed a new layer of soil. She stood listening with bowed head, trying to stifle her yawns. She asked the cleric into the house but he refused the invitation courteously.

When he arrived back at the mosque he was covered in sweat. The door to his wife's room was closed and on the veranda all the blinds had been lowered, enclosing the small space, and the rooms it gave on to, in a cool, tranquil stillness. Waiting for him in his bedroom was the man who made his living by selling spectacles and eye medicine at street corners. He was drinking bright-red cordial from an aluminium tumbler; and as Maulana Hafeez entered, he quickly put out the cigarette he had been drawing on so pleasurably. He put the cigarette in his pocket and stood up to greet the cleric.

'There was no need to hurry,' said Maulana Hafeez. 'You should have waited for the sun to go down a little.'

The vendor responded by making a humble noise at the back of his throat. Maulana Hafeez wiped the oily sweat from his face and the sides of his neck. The vendor set about opening his large leather case; its felt-lined inside was divided into several compartments, all taken up by tidy rows of spectacles. The frames were identical – imitation tortoiseshell – and the glass of the lenses they carried had a greenish tinge. The inside of the lid too was adapted to hold ranks of eye drops, each small vial secured by its neck to a clamp-like, near-complete circle. And there were many compact boxes containing monocles. Maulana Hafeez brought a chair over and sat down facing the man, who immediately began asking him his questions.

Maulana Hafeez answered each question thoughtfully and precisely.

'Myopia,' the optician announced when he had finished the questioning. 'It's also called near-sightedness because things near the eye are less out of focus than those far away.' Maulana Hafeez was nodding uncertainly. 'It's natural, Maulana-ji,' the optician continued. He explained how, due to stiffening with age of certain muscles in the eye, almost everyone lost some ability to see distant objects; and how people who were far-sighted when young had near-perfect vision in their old age because the myopia of their later years counterbalanced, and therefore corrected, the earlier defect.

'God's wisdom is limitless,' responded the cleric. The optician leaned forward in his chair towards Maulana Hafeez and began handing him pairs of glasses.

The blurred edges contracted all of a sudden and objects came sharply into focus – even those that he had thought of as simply too far away to be seen. Maulana Hafeez was taken aback – that others observed things with such clarity, that all the time he too had been meant to see the world as clearly as this.

'This one is just right,' Maulana Hafeez said, looking around and pointing up at the pair resting on his nose. He took them off and carefully folded down the arms. The vendor walked around the case, some of whose neat rows were now in disarray, and began to examine Maulana Hafeez's eyes. Using a forefinger and thumb he exposed almost half of each eyeball and, holding his face inches away from Maulana Hafeez, shone a torch into each eye.

Maulana Hafeez had never seen another face so close to his own. He struggled to look away. 'You didn't have to come straightaway, you could have waited until it was cooler.'

'There's no problem, Maulana-ji,' said the vendor. 'You must provide us sinners with more chances to be of service to you.'

Maulana Hafeez did not hear him; he was not listening. 'A terrible calamity,' he said. 'A tragedy. May he find a place in God's paradise. God is the glorious truth.'

At last, the man stepped back. Maulana Hafeez straightened in his chair.

'A terrible business,' the vendor agreed. He had picked up the small wallet-like case in which the glasses would be stored when not in use. He was preoccupied with dusting it clean, paying especial attention to the area around the clasp. 'This morning when I heard the announcement from . . .' He broke off, looking disconcerted.

But Maulana Hafeez encouraged him to continue with a nod.

'. . . from the *other* mosque, I went straight to the house to see if there was anything I could do, see if I could help with the arrangements.' He placed the chosen spectacles in the wallet, added a square of yellow felt, and snapped shut the clasp.

Maulana Hafeez looked down into his lap. 'It is true. I didn't make the announcement till noon. I didn't think there would be any need.'

The vendor accepted Maulana Hafeez's money – after a flurry of refusals – and was ready to leave. But he lingered over the fastening of his case, and once the case was packed, seemed reluctant to pick it up. 'Maulana-ji,' he said finally, placing a hand on the cleric's forearm. 'There is a reason why I answered your message so quickly. I have to tell you.'

With a faint nod Maulana Hafeez motioned him to retake the seat he had just vacated.

'Maulana-ji,' the man began very quietly, 'when this morning we went to the deputy commissioner's house to give him a message from the police inspector, we saw a girl in his house.'

Maulana Hafeez remained silent for a few moments. He prepared his answer. 'Are you sure? Because those who spread slander will be punished here on earth *and* in the Hereafter. Your own tongue will be called upon to testify against you, about the evil uses to which it was put.'

'Maulana-ji, I saw her myself. We went inside and there she was, combing her hair, with a bottle of linseed oil by her side.' With both forefingers he pointed to his eyes and added: 'With these eyes, Maulana-ji.'

Maulana Hafeez lifted his beard. Again it was some time before he spoke. 'I'll look into it and see what can be done. Azhar is a very good man, there is bound to be an explanation. She was probably a servant.' He rose from the chair, indicating that the exchange was over.

'But in the meantime,' he added, as they reached the front door, 'I must ask you to be discreet. Do not mention this to anyone else.'

Back in his bedroom Maulana Hafeez placed the rosary next to the clock on the shelf and picked up the newspaper lying folded on the bed. Rain had pockmarked the paper and when it crackled it made a sound more crisp than usual. Maulana Hafeez read the newspaper methodically, beginning as always at the top of the front page and working his way down. Occasionally he had to turn to one of the inner pages to continue a front-page story; and this he did by carefully folding and refolding, and counting the columns with a forefinger until he reached the appropriate number. Some of the columns had a few blank spaces where stories of appropriate length had not been found to replace the censored items. Maulana Hafeez glanced at the advertisements and – it was Wednesday – read the children's supplement. There was a photograph of a Japanese robot. Encased in gleaming chromium plates fastened together with rivets, the automaton had the appearance of a human male and could, the caption ran, function like a man.

Maulana Hafeez read until four attuned chimes from the clock in his wife's room told him that soon it would be time for Asar – the third prayers of the day. The heat was beginning to subside. He washed himself with water from the clay pitcher in the bathroom and went into his wife's room. The blinds were still closed and the light in the room was subdued. The woman was saying her rosary.

Maulana Hafeez walked over to the shelf and unscrewed the cap of the attar bottle. The smell of roses quickly spread to his wife's side of the room. 'Tell Mansoor to wait for me when he comes back for the newspaper,' Maulana Hafeez said over his shoulder.

She lowered her beads into her lap. 'He wanted to see you when he brought it over, Maulana-ji. He waited, said he had something to tell you.' And in response to the puzzled look on her husband's face she added: 'It seems there was a woman in the deputy commissioner's house last night.'

There was a silence from Maulana Hafeez. Then, 'Who says so?'

The woman shook her head and shrugged.

Maulana Hafeez transferred the small circle of attar from the tip of his forefinger to his shirt. The cold water he had used for ablutions had comforted the skin on his arms, feet and face but his eyes had remained like two live coals embedded in his skull. 'I've known about it since last week. I saw a woman going into the house at night and I knew a woman had no business going there, especially at night-time. Now I suppose I'll have to talk to him.' He set the attar bottle on the shelf and turned around. 'But in any case I would like a word with Mansoor himself about the television he has brought into his house.'

'Mansoor?' the woman said. 'He is not rich enough to afford a television, Maulana-ji.'

'Precisely,' Maulana Hafeez said, turning his head at an angle. 'Doesn't he realise that he is offending God if he has got himself into debt for something like this?'

'How do you know he has one, Maulana-ji?'

'There's an antenna on the roof of his house,' Maulana Hafeez said coolly. 'I've just seen it from my window.' And with that he reached into his pocket to show his wife his recent purchase.

# *Thursday*

—

Alice pushed the door open with her foot. She was returning from the street corner, clutching three enormous bundles of spinach, the turgid leaves spilling over her elbows. The morning was bright, the sunlight almost tangible, as though the walls were draped in sheets of luminous cloth. Alice stopped at the door to the kitchen and, frowning, looked around. Zébun was on the veranda. She had taken down the calendar from the stretch of wall between the two windows and was turning over the new month two days early.

'What is this smell?' Alice said from the door.

Mr Kasmi was at the kitchen table. He turned and saw the girl. 'Coffee,' he replied, and added in explanation: 'It's like tea. You drink it.'

Alice was familiar with the name of the drink. She wrinkled her nose. 'It smells like stale hookah-water.'

Mr Kasmi smiled broadly. He took a sip from the cup and, after a moment's pause, said, 'So it does. So it does.' Alice gave him a triumphant look. He pointed at the spinach. 'Is all that for us?'

She looked down at the leaves spread across her forearms and gave a nod. She stepped into the kitchen and, unloading the dark-green leaves on the table, considered them once again. 'It looks more than we need,' she agreed, 'but that is because it hasn't been cooked yet. At first they'll fill the pot up to the brim but after five minutes they'll shrivel and go down to this.' She held up her left hand, fingers spread to the size of a small bowl, for Mr Kasmi to see.

Mr Kasmi sipped his coffee. Alice cut the twine and began to pick out the unhealthy leaves. 'I was lucky to get these. It was all they had left,' she said. 'Everything else has gone to Judge

27

Anwar's house. So many people have come since yesterday. There is a row of daigs cooking outside the house.' She closed her eyes and made a mock shudder run through her spine.

Mr Kasmi watched her across the width of the table. He had often thought that the tiny hairs on her small, dark face looked like the symmetrical patterns of magnetised iron-filings. To keep up with fashion her shirt had been lengthened with new material at the bottom and the seam concealed beneath a strip of lace. On her head she created flimsy ringlets by patiently working twigs and matchsticks and bits of wire into her hair at night and securing them with hairpins.

Alice looked up. 'The police are questioning my sister today, because she works in the house.'

Mr Kasmi stood up. 'Well, an insider has to be involved.'

'If it was a case of simple robbery,' Alice said, 'I would question the people who made the cupboards and cabinets, they are usually involved. They tell the robbers what kind of keys they'll need in which house.'

Zébun came into the room. 'What are you talking about, girl?' Her voice was weary. She lowered herself into a chair and fanned herself with the calendar page – it showed a slender woman, an ancient princess, picking flowers from a shrub on whose branches birds sang indifferent to her presence.

Mr Kasmi was smiling as he carried the empty cup to the shelf. 'I think our Alice-bibi has been talking to schoolboys, sister-ji,' he said over his shoulder. 'Next she'll be telling us that to hold loot thieves have extra-deep pockets sewn into their trousers.'

Zébun put down the page and began slowly to undo her hair, picking with her fingertips at the knot of the ribbon. 'I still can't believe he's dead,' she said, unweaving her wiry grey plait. 'I saw him walk by the window on Sunday. Little did I know that I was seeing him for the last time.'

Mr Kasmi picked up the small jar of coffee from the shelf. He turned to Alice and said, 'The woman we had before you used to say on hearing about someone's death, What is there to a human being? Nothing but illusions.' Then, including Zébun in his gaze he said, 'Do you remember, sister-ji?'

Zébun gave a nod. With smooth, flowing strokes she dragged the comb through her hair. Any loose hairs she carefully wrapped around her forefinger and collected in her lap. Alice stretched across the table and picked up the torn calendar page. 'Can I have it? I told you I liked it a lot.'

The sun was still low when Mr Kasmi stepped out of the house. The heat had not yet begun. The streets were in shadow. Mr Kasmi set off slowly in the direction of the school. There had been just two prolonged showers in the previous two days, but already seeds were beginning to germinate along the edges of the streets and the lower parts of the houses looked as though they had been dusted in a fine, green powder – the beginnings of what would become, within two weeks of the monsoon's arrival, a pelt of velvety moss.

Azhar was leaving his house. His recently washed hair was slicked back away from his forehead. He saw Mr Kasmi, and raised his hand and smiled. Mr Kasmi waved back from his side of the street. Azhar strode away in the opposite direction. Within the next few minutes Mr Kasmi could see the school, a charmless building. Ten yards further on and he began to catch whiffs of the penetrating odour that the newer parts of the building gave off in the rainy season.

Mr Kasmi had once taught here. In those days the school consisted of one room, serving as headmaster's office and staff room, and a walled-in strip of level ground where lessons were given by the three teachers to boys who sat cross-legged on the grass. Summer holidays would begin on the day a pupil passed out from the sun. Mr Kasmi's had been the first bicycle in town, and the sight of his gangling frame riding in through the gate the first morning had caused a sensation. The wheels left behind two wavy lines in the mud, like the path of two butterflies chasing each other in early March. Since Mr Kasmi's retirement, however, three new rooms had been added to the building. The pond behind the old room was drained and people were asked to dump their rubbish into the enormous crater left behind. Four months later cement was poured over the garbage and the new rooms were built.

Making unsuccessful attempts at breathing through his mouth, Mr Kasmi entered the small corridor at the end of which was the headmaster's office. Two classrooms faced on to the corridor. The headmaster was not in his office. Mr Kasmi dusted the moulded plastic chair and, propping his small zip-up bag against a leg of the chair, sat down to wait. Opposite him – through the open door and across the corridor – the teacher had returned to the classroom and the monitor, a pale-skinned boy with delicate gestures, was presenting him with the names of boys who had misbehaved in his absence. The monitor returned quietly to his seat, the bench nearest to the teacher's chair. The names were called out. Mr Kasmi watched, handkerchief pressed to his nose, as two boys got up and walked slowly to the front of the room. Before settling in his chair the teacher said something to the two boys which Mr Kasmi was too far away to catch clearly. They stood motionless for a few moments, facing each other. Then, prompted by a shout from the teacher, the taller of the pair reached out his hand and struck the other boy's face – the shallow arc of the splayed palm made a sharp sound on impact. Mr Kasmi stood up. The boy who had been hit swung his arm to catch the other's face. But the blow was foiled – the taller boy dipped his head sideways and, straightening, slapped the other boy's face once again. Mr Kasmi looked around; he had forgotten the bad smell. Another blow was struck and – perhaps Mr Kasmi had been seen – a boy walked up and closed the classroom door.

Mr Kasmi remained motionless for a few moments. Then, pressing the handkerchief to his nose, he sat down. He closed his eyes to calm his heartbeat.

'A new month, Kasmi-sahib,' said the headmaster. He stood in the doorway, smiling across the room at Mr Kasmi. Mr Kasmi returned the smile.

A wave of the foul smell rose from beneath the floor.

'You get used to it, Kasmi-sahib,' the headmaster said cheerfully, pointing at Mr Kasmi's handkerchief. He had walked around his desk and was settled in his chair. A little embarrassed, Mr Kasmi returned the handkerchief to his pocket. He unzipped his bag and took out the pension book.

As he handed the stamped book back across the desk the headmaster shook his head mockingly and said, 'I'm a generous man, Kasmi-sahib. I keep giving you all this money despite the fact that even with a double MA you don't know anything about literature.'

Mr Kasmi shut his eyelids and, raising a forefinger, whispered an 'ah'. He smiled. This was a long-standing but friendly argument. Mr Kasmi had always believed that Chaucer's *Squiere's Tale* was based on a story from the *Arabian Nights*, taken to Europe by Italian merchants from the Black Sea. The headmaster never accepted this. He did not even acknowledge the similarity between the two stories. To back up his argument Mr Kasmi would bring back pages of notes every time he visited a city library. The headmaster would give them a cursory glance and say, 'No. Chaucer is far superior. Far, far superior.'

Stepping out of the office, Mr Kasmi strained to catch any noises coming from the classroom in front of him. Then he shook his head; there was no reason to suppose that the duel was still going on.

Mr Kasmi unhooked one leaf of the school gate and emerged on to the street. The sun shone oppressively, producing in the sky a glare so brilliant that it ate into the silhouettes, blurring their edges. The heat was beginning. The fortnightly queue of labourers was in place outside Mujeeb Ali's house, winding around the walls and stretching out of sight behind a cluster of trees. A few of the men had broken away and were helping to restrain a headstrong mare, kicking up dust. The others watched with interest, shouting occasional words of advice and encouragement. Mr Kasmi waited under a tree for the beast to be overpowered before resuming his walk towards the courthouse. He went along the riverbank, passing the bus station which was deserted at this hour. A bus remained in the shelter at all times, parked with its muzzle pressed against the posts. At seven o'clock every morning a busload of people, animals and birds, boxes and crates left the stand; to be replaced, an hour or so later, by the incoming service bringing the mail, newspapers, and schoolboys from the surrounding villages, as well as other passengers. There was another exchange in the evenings.

Mr Kasmi went to Yusuf Rao's office. The small room stood away from the other buildings of the courthouse in the shadow of a dusty jand tree. The area around the giant tree's roots was overwhelmed by weeds that had run to seed and were turning yellow.

'Waiting for customers?' Mr Kasmi said into the office before entering. Above him hung a small, clumsily painted sign–

### YUSUF RAO.
#### ADVOCATE, NOTARY-PUBLIC,
#### NON-OFFICIAL JAIL VISITOR

The room was approximately twenty feet by ten; and pushed against the longer wall, behind the desk and beneath the only window, was a narrow rope cot on which Yusuf Rao was lying, his hands clasped behind his neck, his eyes closed.

'Of course.' Yusuf Rao opened his eyes. 'Lawyers are like prostitutes. If a customer comes we eat, otherwise we go hungry.' He swung his feet to the floor and felt for his slippers.

Mr Kasmi approached the desk. 'The courts are shut for four days in honour of the judge but I knew you'd still be here, waiting to pounce on some unfortunate passer-by.' Through the open window he could see the empty arches of the courthouse and, brilliant-white in the sunshine, the whitewashed bricks that lined the edges of the paths leading to various parts of the building. Yusuf Rao, because he had been the first lawyer in town, was the only one who had managed to build an office. The three younger lawyers conducted their business from kiosks which stood beneath the trees. Their signs were chained and padlocked against those who would steal them for roofing material.

With an effort Yusuf Rao got to his feet and stiffly took the three steps to his desk. 'I'm an optimist. Anything's possible in a country where the land reforms are welcomed by the landowners.'

'And while we're on the subject of the rich,' Mr Kasmi said seriously, 'who do you think it was? About the judge, I mean.'

Yusuf Rao drummed his fingers on the desk. 'I don't know. He was a judge, corrupt to the core. *And* he was involved in politics. It could be anyone.'

Many years before, having just returned to the town of his birth to begin a practice, Yusuf Rao had soon understood that Judge Anwar of the Fourth Criminal Court put many obstacles in the way of justice. He had duly denounced the judge to the authorities in the capital, accusing him of failing to remand known criminals, even murderers, in custody and allowing them to intimidate witnesses; he had also given court credentials to some of the killers on the Special Commission's list.

'*And* he was rich,' Mr Kasmi said, unfastening his bag.

'Yes, but they didn't take anything. They must have come with only one thing on their mind.' Yusuf Rao touched two fingers to his right temple.

Mr Kasmi took out the jar of coffee.

'Coffee!' Yusuf Rao exclaimed and finished taming his hair with the palms of his hand. He leaned forward and took the jar from Mr Kasmi's hand. 'Where did you get it?'

Mr Kasmi studied the pleasure on his friend's face. 'Burkat's wife brought it. She came to see me on Tuesday, wanted me to write a letter in English to her son.'

Yusuf Rao was drawing the smell of the grounds into his nostrils. 'Yes. I heard she was back from Canada.'

Mr Kasmi said, cautiously, 'She's Kalsum's sister. Did you know that?'

Yusuf Rao nodded without looking up. 'Yes, I did.' And replacing the lid on the jar he asked, 'How is that poor woman?'

'She gets by,' Mr Kasmi replied. 'After the boy died Mujeeb Ali went on paying her his wages. She's grateful for that.'

Yusuf Rao's head shot up. 'Is she, really?' He smiled with one side of his mouth. 'Perhaps someone should tell her that it was Mujeeb Ali who had her boy murdered in the first place.'

'There's no evidence for that. That is only your theory.'

Yusuf Rao ignored the interruption. 'A neat arrangement. I get my eighteen-year-old employee to fire at my political opponent at an election meeting. And to cover up I hire assassins to beat the boy to death after he has fired the shot. My opponent has a hole in his thigh, the boy is dead, and I get a chance every month to prove my generosity by giving money to the boy's mother. A very neat arrangement indeed.'

In the past on more than one occasion Mr Kasmi and Yusuf Rao had discussed this matter much more passionately, both men refusing to give ground. But today Mr Kasmi just shrugged. 'How is your leg, anyway?'

'The bones in my hip grind against each other like a mortar against a pestle.' Yusuf Rao had measured out two generous pinches of the coffee grounds on to a sheet of yellow typing paper and was wrapping it up, folding the paper into a compact diamond shape.

The sun was climbing fast. The patch of sunlight which was on the floor when Mr Kasmi arrived had crept on to the desktop, illuminating the crescents of dried tea left by cups and saucers. The heat in the small, cramped office was intense. The small pedestal fan set on top of the filing cabinet, its lead disappearing under the rope cot, spun noisily. Mr Kasmi wiped his brow. 'Not for me,' he gestured towards the coffee. 'I have to go to the post office before it closes to draw my pension.'

But Yusuf waved his objection aside. He walked to the door and shouted for the boy at the tea-stall across the street. He was supporting himself against the doorframe with one hand and brandished the packet of coffee above his head to attract attention.

After giving the boy detailed instructions on how to prepare the drink he came back and, with a grimace of discomfort, settled in the swivel chair. 'In 1951, the prime minister was assassinated

34

in exactly the same way. The man who fired the shot was beaten to death then and there. The newspapers said it was the enraged crowd but the whole country knows that that was not the case.'

Indifferent to the shouts of protest and working free of the arms that tried to hold him back, the old man detached himself from the group of men wedged in the door and entered the room. He advanced towards the desk behind which the overseer and the clerk sat and began cursing in a loud voice. The men behind the desk watched him calmly through narrowing eyes. The clerk folded his arms over the ledger. Ranged on the desk in neat stacks were coins and bundles of banknotes. The words *increase productivity* appeared on the coins and the notes of lower denomination.

'What's the matter?' The door at the rear end of the room opened and Mujeeb Ali stepped in, followed by Azhar. The crowd at the street door fell silent. Both the overseer and the clerk struggled to sit up straight.

The old man, covered in sweat, turned to Mujeeb Ali. 'I've been standing in the sun all day because he refuses to pay my wages,' he said in a gravelly voice. Beneath the wrinkles on his neck the cartilage rings of his windpipe could be made out.

'Wait for your turn,' Mujeeb Ali said. 'It can't be long now.'

'My turn has come and gone,' protested the old man. 'He says I'll be the last one to get paid because I'm impertinent.'

Mujeeb Ali glanced at the overseer. The clerk had turned back several pages and was searching feverishly for the old man's name.

The old peasant took two steps towards Mujeeb Ali. 'He didn't want me to sit in the shade. He said I'd ruin the grass in your garden. So I asked him if he thought I had a sickle for an arse. That's all I said.'

Azhar threw back his head and let out a laugh. 'Sickle for an arse. That's good,' he said to the old man. But the peasant, debilitated by hunger and the heat, stared in silence.

After making a thumbprint in the ledger and collecting his wages the old man went towards the door. At the threshold he stopped, took off his turban and wiped his face. A few dishevelled strands of silvery hair stood on his otherwise bald head. Then he turned and looked boldly at Mujeeb Ali. 'I've worked on your lands since the days of your grandfather,' he said and stepped out on to the street.

As the overseer and the clerk leafed back to their former place in the ledger, Mujeeb Ali led Azhar to the other end of the room. It was the only room in the large house that faced the street. The entire length of one wall was given over to the framed photographs, large and small, of several generations of the Ali family's male members. It was said that when Sher Bahadar Ali, Mujeeb's grandfather, died his two sons had divided the inheritance – silver and gold and money – using shovels and a balance from the stables. Mujeeb Ali and both his brothers had inherited the powerful shoulders and arms of their father. In several photographs Mujeeb Ali's youngest brother appeared, at various ages, with a bird of prey perched on a fist. And there was one photograph of the three brothers together, arms around garlanded shoulders, taken on the day following the last general election.

Azhar and Mujeeb Ali stood by the open window. Mujeeb Ali asked Azhar about the investigations into the judge's death. Azhar confessed that the police did not have a single piece of evidence which could suggest a line of inquiry. When the police were called in, shortly after dawn the day before, the inspector had stationed sergeants in all the principal streets; and at daybreak volunteers had combed the long approaches into the town, but the murderers had left behind no clues. 'Do you remember the murder last month when the woman's secret yaar broke in and killed the husband,' Azhar said, and without waiting for an answer continued: 'Well, last night the police inspector had to intervene when the judge's wife's brothers beat up a man who suggested that perhaps the two cases were similar.'

Azhar had, he said, appointed himself the examining magistrate, which meant that as well as exercising the familiar judicial

prerogative of putting people in jail, he was responsible for collecting evidence and conducting investigations. In principle he
had to gather all the facts relating to the death, weigh them up
with proper objectivity, and determine whether a case should
proceed. And he had decided to start by looking at some of the
recent cases Judge Anwar had presided over, and interviewing
the relevant people.

At the other end of the room the clerk had begun setting the
desk in order. The overseer crossed the room towards Mujeeb
Ali and Azhar. Mujeeb Ali took out a bunch of keys from his
pocket, his thick index finger looped round the brass ring.

'Everyone in the world, it seems, is talking about the
judge-sahib's murder,' the overseer said as he drew close, 'and
those letters.' He carried a stack of ledgers, narrow and thick,
balanced on the top of which were rolls of banknotes secured
with orange rubber-bands and several packets of coins. Now
that his task had been completed he appeared less tense. 'Most
of these people' – he nodded towards the street door – 'have
never received a letter in their lives, but today even they
mentioned them.'

Azhar turned his back to the open window. 'I have heard a
journalist is coming from the capital in a day or two to write up
the story of those letters.'

Mujeeb Ali and the overseer were walking away from him.
The overseer said over his shoulder to Azhar, 'A woman whose
son ran away from home twenty years ago says she dreamt last
night that one of the letters is going to be from him.'

Azhar lit a cigarette and turned back to the window. He
glanced across the vast backyard paved with chessboard tiles.
The town was at the confluence of two of the province's five
rivers and Mujeeb Ali's house stood in sight of the eastern
branch. The interfluvial plain was considered the richest agri-
cultural land in the country. And here most of it – orchards,
vineyards, cornfields, rice-paddies – belonged to the Alis. On
three sides, Mujeeb Ali had reminded a gathering during the
run-up to the last elections, you are surrounded by water and on

the fourth side is my family's land; so if you won't support us I will drive you into the water.

Azhar flicked the cigarette on to the baking tiles and walked over to the other side of the room. The overseer and the clerk had taken their leave. Mujeeb Ali turned the key in the armoured cupboard embedded in the wall; a portrait of the Founder of the state hung above it.

'I'll start looking into the files when the courts open on Sunday,' Azhar said. 'I'll be away till Saturday.'

Mujeeb Ali accompanied him to the door. Azhar went towards the street where Dr Sharif lived to deliver a message from the judge's widow: the physician was to call at the house and collect any of the dead man's medicines he thought he could use. Mujeeb Ali watched him cross the street – as he stepped into shade the glare of his spotless white shirt was extinguished. Mujeeb Ali bolted the door. In the absence of any noise the room appeared more spacious and, since the sunlight too had been excluded, it felt cooler. The only reminder of the manic activity of the past few hours was a faint smell of human sweat clinging to the walls. Mujeeb Ali went into the house through the rear door.

The courtyard, a square expanse of ochre terrazzo, was enclosed on three sides by shallow verandas and bound on the fourth side by alternating male and female pawpaws, jasmine bushes and domestic palms whose tips had been clipped to give them the appearance of Japanese fans. Mujeeb Ali crossed the courtyard, picking his way around the fruit and vegetables that had been spread out by the servant women on sheets of white cloth to dry in the sun. There were sections of mango, salted green chilli and lady's finger with slits along the length for the pickles; carrots, apples and cubes of pumpkin for the preserves; plums and pods of tamarind for the chutneys. The season's beans and pulses had been ground, moistened with milk and worked into coin-sized tablets for the winter months.

'I wish it would rain,' Mujeeb Ali said, entering the bedroom. 'After all, it is supposed to be the rainy season.'

Nabila Ali did not acknowledge him. Reclining against the pillows, she continued to read from the velvet-bound copy of *Bahishti Zévar* which, according to custom, she had received in her dowry. The fabric had long since lost its shine and the edges were torn. Nabila's hair, still hot as metal from the street – she had just returned from Judge Anwar's house – was loose on her shoulders. Mujeeb Ali cleared his throat and sat down on the edge of the bed. He made the noise again.

Nabila lowered the book. It was a full minute before she spoke. 'You, ji, may not have any fear of God left in you, but I still do,' she said in a determined tone.

Mujeeb Ali made as if to speak but changed his mind. Nabila sat up and placed the book on the night-table beside the bed. 'It's a sin even to offer food to a fornicator.' She had stood up. 'Even a mother is supposed to refuse food to her son if she suspects him of . . .' She left the sentence unfinished, completing it with a wave of her hand.

Mujeeb Ali followed her with his eyes as she crossed to the wardrobe. 'What do you want me to do about it?' he asked quietly, undoing his shirt.

Nabila had opened one side of the wardrobe and was taking out a change of clothes for her husband. White muslin shirts and linen trousers were arranged neatly on the shelves. Each garment bore the small indelible insignia that the laundryman had assigned to the household. 'You, ji, seem to have forgotten that we have daughters in the house.' Every time she spoke passionately the vein on the left side of Nabila's neck swelled up. After a brief pause she added: 'And that we are also responsible for the safety and honour of the servant girls.'

Mujeeb Ali nodded. 'She's a Christian, isn't she?'

Nabila's glance yielded at last. She looked at her husband and said quietly: 'Elizabeth Massih.'

Mujeeb Ali unbuckled the belt that held the holster under his left arm and, with the revolver resting by his side on the bed, he took off his vest. 'What do you want me to do?'

'Stop inviting him into the house. Deputy commissioner or no deputy commissioner, I don't want any sinners in my house.'

'How do you know her name?'

Nabila closed the wardrobe after making sure that nothing inside would catch in the door. 'All the women were talking about it.' There were sharp creases in the fabric of her tunic running across the stomach, caused by her having spent the last few hours sitting cross-legged, praying for the repose of the dead man's soul.

'How is Asgri today?'

Nabila heaved a sigh and lowered herself onto the edge of the bed. 'Everyone knows that crying never brought anyone back but what else can she do?' She was twisting her hair into a bun.

'They'll be caught,' Mujeeb Ali said matter-of-factly and sat down two places away from his wife. He picked up the shirt he had taken off and began to clean his shoes with it.

Nabila was securing her hair into place; she held the hairpins between her teeth. She took out the last one and said, 'Parveen Shafiq says that she was washing herself for the dawn prayers when she heard someone running past her bathroom window.'

Mujeeb Ali gave a nod. 'We'll see what can be done.' He felt for the keys in the old shirt.

'Remember, ji,' said Nabila, 'I don't want him in this house any more.'

Mujeeb Ali looked back from the door. 'I'll be back about this time tomorrow,' and he left the house without acknowledging the greetings of the servant women who were returning for the evening, having spent the afternoon with their families.

The ticking of the clock was a clear, precise sound in Nabila's head. She was thinking about Asgri. Shortly after daybreak the previous Monday – before the servants began arriving and the children were awoken – Nabila had answered the door to find a distraught Asgri standing at the doorstep. Her fingers seemed to tremble. 'I want you to take me to the Clinic,' she had said in a voice that betrayed a night without sleep. Nabila had taken her into the kitchen. 'I pleaded with him to leave me alone just for tonight, but he wouldn't listen, Nabila,' she said through tears. 'I don't want another one at my age. And anyway, it will probably be a girl again. I don't have to explain anything to you – you have five girls of your own. Only Allah Himself knows why He has decided to punish us both this way. Take me to the Clinic.' As a pretext for calling at her friend's house at such an early hour – a pretext thoroughly unconvincing – she had brought an empty flour bowl.

Maulana Hafeez transferred the folded newspaper to his other armpit and knocked on the door. Above him bird-droppings had caused a tomato plant to germinate between two loose bricks. The walls of the small house were streaked with broad vertical bands of lichen. During the summer months the sun would scorch this lichen, turning its lush green to a dull grey, but the monsoon always restored these stripes to the poor people's houses. Maulana Hafeez knocked again.

Mansoor's wife, her face painted pink with cosmetics, came to the door. To numb a headache she had tied her stole tightly around her head. 'Maulana-ji!' she said, reaching behind her ears to untie the knot in the stole. Then, on noticing the newspaper, she said, 'You shouldn't have troubled yourself, Maulana-ji. Mansoor would have collected it himself.'

She dutifully covered her head and chest with the stole and backed on to the narrow courtyard to allow Maulana Hafeez into the house.

Mansoor sat on the edge of the bed, eating. He raised each mouthful – a well-worked ball of rice and lentils – on the fingers of his right hand and guided it into his mouth with the thumb. At the other end of the small room the television set gave off a bluish-white glow. Ranged around the set, their heads tilted backwards, were about a dozen of the neighbourhood's children. Most of them were half-naked – taut stomachs swelling up beneath xylophone ribcages. They were watching a violently energetic cartoon.

Mansoor stood up when his wife entered the room followed by Maulana Hafeez. With his shins he pushed away the small table on which his meal was set. His exuberant adam's apple and long neck made him look like an estuary bird. 'You shouldn't have troubled yourself, Maulana-ji.'

Since his right hand was greasy from the food Mansoor offered Maulana Hafeez his right forearm. His wife meanwhile had switched off the television and voltage stabiliser, and was quietly asking the children to leave. They left in silence but from the street their excited voices reached the room.

The cleric insisted Mansoor continue with his meal. Mansoor repeated his half-hearted greeting and sat down.

Staring into his lap where the tips of his fingers were engaged with the beads of the rosary that Mujeeb Ali had brought back for him from Mecca, without further preamble Maulana Hafeez revealed the real reason for the visit.

'On the outskirts of every town in this province there is a cinema which shows immoral, indecent and sinful pictures.' Between each adjective Maulana Hafeez paused for a few seconds. 'However, it is our good fortune that the God-fearing citizens of this town, in collaboration with the diligent people who have influence over such matters, have made sure that no such establishment be permitted to take root here.'

For over a fortnight Mansoor had been expecting a visit from Maulana Hafeez. He chewed quietly on a sliver of raw onion.

'It would seem that all their good work was pointless,' Maulana Hafeez said. 'Because we can now, if we so wish, turn our *homes* into little cinemas.'

Mansoor's wife came in, stirring sugar into a glass of lemon water, and with an anxious glance at her husband presented the drink to the cleric. He accepted gratefully and drank – keeping to the Strictures – in a succession of three short sips.

Mansoor said, 'Forgive me, Maulana-ji, but a television programme is not the same as a cinema film.'

'That is irrelevant.' Maulana Hafeez closed his eyes. 'If something is forbidden, it is forbidden. You only need a *pinch* of poison.'

Mansoor explained how the transmission began and ended each day with a recitation from the Qur'an, and how since the new religious measures by the regime the programmes broke off at prayer time. These intermissions were long enough to allow men to make their way to the nearest mosque, discouraging them from praying at home like women.

But the maulana was shaking his head. 'In my opinion,' he said to his lap, 'this will lead to other, more serious, neglect of the rules laid down by Hazrat Muhammad *sallula-hé-valla-hé-vasalum*.'

On hearing the Prophet's name, the woman kissed the tips of her fingers and lightly touched them to her eyes. 'I don't understand what you mean, Maulana-ji,' she said irritably: the stole which she had been using before Maulana Hafeez's arrival to numb her headache was now back in place, covering her head and the upper part of her body, and the headache had resurfaced.

Maulana Hafeez looked up. The woman was standing by a shelf at the other side of the room. He reached into his pocket – the movement released the smell of attar from the folds of his shirt – and pulled out his glasses. On the shelf there were many framed samplers with verses from the Qur'an, and in a soda bottle filled with water a shoot of vine had thrown long hairy roots which looked like rats' tails. The shelf was draped in white cloth embroidered with colourful bouquets and fragments from the poems of Wamaq Saleem. There was a photograph of a very young man, not much more than a boy, standing against the backdrop of clear blue sky.

'Your guard has already been lowered,' Maulana Hafeez said. 'There was a time when a death in the area meant no one celebrated Eid that year. Now I see that with the dead man's shroud not yet soiled in the grave you were entertaining yourselves.' And bowed like a crescent on the edge of the bed, he repeated quietly: 'Your guard has already been lowered, my dhi.'

'But we were doing it privately, Maulana-ji,' the woman said, ignoring the angry glances from her husband. Her face was pink with powder but the skin on her neck showed dark brown.

'That is precisely where the danger lies,' Maulana Hafeez said, visibly disappointed, 'in this talk of privacy. It causes people to become selfish, and will lead to the founding of a morally base society.'

Mansoor raised his hand and nodded. 'I realise that I was wrong to switch it on so soon after the death, but, with respect, Maulana-ji, you seem to be suggesting that mine is the only television in the town.'

The woman said: 'Far worse things go on behind the walls of the bigger houses, Maulana-ji. The very night they kill the judge for being corrupt the town finds a woman in the deputy commissioner's house.'

Mansoor looked sharply at his wife.

But Maulana Hafeez placed a hand on his arm. Then he looked at the woman and said, 'You'd better go into the other room, my dhi.'

She left in silence.

Maulana Hafeez took a succession of deep breaths but failed to locate the smell of roses. 'The deeds of others are not our concern. We must dedicate our lives to the pursuit of moral and religious excellence.' The tips of his fingers, smudged with newspaper ink, slid a bead along his rosary every few seconds.

The call for prayers from the other mosque – the denomination called its followers twenty minutes before Maulana Hafeez – alerted him to the time. He noticed that he had drained his glass. 'The days are getting shorter. It'll be time for Magrib soon,' he said, and stood up with considerable effort. During the rains his muscles felt as though they had developed knots along their lengths.

Dusk had fallen. Bats were out and fluttered above the courtyard. 'I sincerely hope you will think about what I've been saying,' Maulana Hafeez said to Mansoor who had accompanied him to the door. 'My privilege is simply to warn people of the dangers of straying on to the wrong path, I don't have the authority or the means of *preventing* them from doing so.'

*An unfamiliar room becomes larger once you get used to it. Nusrat's husband died in this room, peacefully in his sleep – a filament losing its*

*glow over a period of time. The trees in the outside garden reach up to*
*pluck a few notes from the balcony railing.*

*A butterfly alights and becomes one with its shadow, like when you*
*make the tips of your forefinger and thumb touch each other. Nusrat*
*sings:*

> Eggs and their shells.
> Once all the butterflies were white,
> One day, too tired to fly,
> They fell asleep on a flowerbed
> And the dew stained their wings
> With the colours of the petals.

*Winter and summer she wears an old sleeveless jumper, the blue of*
*tattoos. 'My Afghanistani ayah taught me that poem,' she tells us. Her*
*father was personal physician to the emperor of Afghanistan, long long*
*ago. 'He was a doctor,' she makes clear; and proudly: 'Imagine, an FRCS*
*in those days!' The pomegranate in the courtyard is from Kundahar. The*
*sapling was smuggled into the country through the Khyber Pass.*
*'Others were bringing in pearls and' – a quick glance to either side,*
*offering us both her profiles – 'alcohol. But I only brought in a plant.'*
*She laughs at the moulded ceiling. A pomegranate blossom is leathery,*
*resembles a pitcher, and is orange in colour, the intense orange of the*
*back of mirrors. She produces a photograph of her mother. The woman's*
*hairline is hidden beneath a row-of-coins headdress; she sits on a round*
*stone by the fanfare of a trumpet vine. Mother and daughter look alike –*
*their profiles would fit into each other as snugly as two teaspoons.*
*Nusrat's brother died of wasp bites. Ina lila hé va ina ilia é rajeon. He*
*collapsed into a flowerbed with his mouth open. When they lifted him up*
*they saw that a tiny daisy had been enclosed, unharmed, inside the open*
*mouth. 'Once a month we'd both be taken to the cinema,' she remem-*
*bers, bringing to life with words the crowded cinema theatre where*
*smoke from the cigarettes rose to catch, like latecomers, bits of the pro-*
*jection on itself. And they had owned a gramophone with an elbowed*
*limb to carry the needle. Nusrat's marriage forced her to change coun-*
*tries. She bade farewell to the sound of the walnut sellers, méva vendors*
*and bearfights degenerating into bloody brawls, and to the rattle of*

*weapons being tested by potential customers in the gunshop behind the mansion; and she crossed the border to the west.*

*She offers us dates and lumps of holy soil to eat and spoonfuls of the water of Zumzum to drink.*

*Poplar pollen floats in the still air. A few of Nusrat's cats sit in the sunlight, washing themselves. Others stitch their way through our legs, incorporating us – crosswise and lengthwise – into their invisible embroidery; the pattern also includes tables and chairs, the pillars of the veranda and the top branches of the Afghanistani tree. They are given boiled offal to eat twice a day. They cannot digest it uncooked. Someone had once asked, 'Why don't they run away?' Nusrat had smiled: 'They can't. They get their favourite food here.'*

*'It's all ruined, no doubt, since the Russian invasion.' She runs a fingertip along the rim of her eye and harvests a tear. 'You hear about it in the news every day. All those refugees . . .' She gives a heavy sigh and the hairs of her nostrils are visible for a brief moment. Aunt Khursheed sympathises: 'No doubt, no doubt. Things change. It was the same with us. When we went back to India it was all so different. When they announced that there was going to be a partition, no one took it seriously. We left our horses and mules with a neighbour. A Hindu. Everyone thought it was a temporary division and that one day India and Pakistan would be a united country again. But . . .' Aunt Khursheed and her husband had gone back to the place of their birth some years ago and had been unable to recognise the old street, let alone their house. The talli in the courtyard had been cut down; they found the trunk set by the outside wall. Around one of the boughs, Aunt Khursheed recalls with sadness, were two loops of rope: the decaying remains of a swing they had put up as children. She tells Nusrat of the journey they had made following the announcement of Partition, the pilgrimage they had undertaken across the bloody August of 1947. 'We were followed by Sikhs who held in their hands moons dripping with blood.' Her features contract in pain, her eyebrows are tense as bows. 'Savages!'*

*To this, Irfan, her eldest son, would have replied, 'That is not true. Hindus and Sikhs did not harm any emigrating Muslims. Not until the Muslims of this area, the area that is now Pakistan, slaughtered a trainload of Hindus and Sikhs going in the opposite direction, from Rawalpindi to Amritsar.' He is constantly quarrelling with his parents. On the night before the last elections they had stayed up till three o'clock, arguing. In the morning Irfan had left the house without breakfast, before anyone else was awake, and did not come home till the fireflies. He was born on a pile of corpses as his parents were fleeing the massacre.*

*A bushel of peacock feathers standing in a vase on a chest of drawers watches the open door with twenty-four wide-open eyes. A kitten discovers a place never before visited and tries out new echoes.*

*Aunt Khursheed pushes out her elbows and stands up. Nusrat says, 'Tell brother-ji it was very neighbourly of him to think about my well-being, but I don't have any relatives alive.'*

*Outside, Aunt Khursheed whispers to us, 'She may not have anyone now, but wait till she falls ill. Each day will see a new chacha-zad brother standing at the doorstep with a basket of langra mangoes. The house alone is worth thousands.'*

# Saturday

—

Five dry months had altered considerably the form, appearance and character of life in the town. The rains arrived at last on the night of the judge's murder, catching many women unawares with their washing left out on the lines overnight. Thursday night was suffocating but – the monsoon *had* arrived – at noon on Friday the rains returned in force. The servant girls spent most of that evening sterilising with turpentine the many puddles that formed outside the houses. The infernal winds of June and July had exterminated almost all of the insects hatched in April but with the rains came the threat of another wave of mosquitoes.

'I've discovered a flaw in the Maulana-ji's argument,' Azhar whispered, bringing his mouth up to Elizabeth's ear.

Elizabeth opened an eye on to the dunes and caves of the dishevelled sheet – the other still buried in the pillow – and mumbled something incomprehensible to Azhar. She reached out her hand and running a finger along Azhar's spine felt for the place on his back where an over-active follicle had produced a lone curved hair.

'Here's the join,' said Azhar, touching the ridge of skin between Elizabeth's legs.

With a little moan of pleasure and the words 'You have no shame', Elizabeth slapped Azhar's back gently.

Yesterday in his Friday sermon Maulana Dawood, having no doubt read the article on the Japanese robot in Wednesday's newspaper, had denounced all 'misguided mortals' who attempted to mimic the 'Almighty's adroitness'. 'Allah's curse on science and the scientists!' He had taken great joy in the fact that whereas the robot was covered in riveted joins, the human body was free of such imperfections.

The pink haze of early morning was clinging to the edges of the objects in the room and outside a mournful drizzle was falling on the houses. Azhar stood in front of the mirror and, squeezing toothpaste directly on to his tongue, began to clean his teeth. During the brief pauses in the brushing he could hear Elizabeth humming to herself as she moved about the bedroom getting dressed. In her speech he would frequently catch fragments of this singing-voice.

She stood at the window looking out. Her hair she had tied with a ribbon and in her ears she wore tiny gold roses. In the trees and under the eaves of the silent houses clusters of sparrows were huddled together, their feathers fluffed into soft masses as they waited for the rain to clear. 'So much rain,' Elizabeth said at the sound of the bathroom door opening. 'At this rate we'll have to lift the town at one end to drain all the water from the houses.'

A set of clean clothes was laid out on the bed and Azhar began to dress in silence. He was young and muscular and his eyes sparkled with good health. He had a delicate triangular chin and Elizabeth had often wondered why its skin did not register the dimple she could so clearly feel in its bone.

'Why are you questioning my father?' she asked quietly. She had turned around and stood facing him.

'Your father?'

'Benjamin Massih is my father,' she said. 'He's broken a leg, yet they still dragged him in for questions yesterday.'

Azhar continued dressing. 'There has to be an accomplice. An insider.'

The response was quick and defiant. 'All he does is unblock the gutters and drains in that street. Why should he be a suspect just because he's familiar with the inside of the house? That makes *you* a suspect as well.'

In the brief silence which followed Azhar buttoned up his shirt. 'We're questioning *all* the servants, Christians and Muslims.'

Unsatisfied, she turned back to the open window.

'This shirt is missing a button,' Azhar exclaimed. 'Look,' he pointed to his chest.

'Take it off,' Elizabeth said, and without a glance in Azhar's direction crossed the room and began to look for the needle and thread.

When she turned around Azhar had still not removed the shirt. 'Why don't you do it while I'm inside it?' He opened his arms.

With a smile she looked away. 'You watch too many films.' She crossed her arms. 'Now take it off.'

Azhar gave a mock sigh, undid the row of buttons and playfully tossed the shirt across the room at Elizabeth. She stretched out her arm and caught it.

Not many hours later, their breakfast was interrupted by three short rings at the front door. Azhar clicked his tongue in irritation – it was the first day of the week and he had been hoping to leave the town earlier than usual. As he stood he frowned at Elizabeth, mocking the concern on her face – she had stopped eating and was looking anxiously in the direction of the sound.

The moment Azhar opened the door the short skinny man standing on the portico straightened to attention. His extremely dark skin was the first thing Azhar registered. An umbrella was still open above the man's head, a drop forming at each angle of the octagon. On the floor by his feet was set a small cardboard suitcase tied with a rope. 'I'm sorry to trouble you so early but I need some directions,' he said, searching in his pocket with the free hand.

'Look . . .' Azhar raised a hand.

'I've been knocking on doors and windows for the past three hours, but no one opened up to help me.'

'We've had a death in town,' Azhar said; and then, to avoid any time-consuming questions, he quickly asked, 'Who are you looking for?'

The man smiled a broad scatter of brilliant white teeth, and produced a neatly folded piece of paper from one of his pockets.

The ink was beginning to dissolve. 'I don't know him,' Azhar said. 'I haven't lived here all that long myself.' And handing back the address he suggested: 'Either wait for the shops to open or go to one of the mosques. One's this way and the other is at the end of the next street.'

The man moved closer. 'Actually, it's this man's wife I've come looking for.' He said with a smile of complicity, 'She's beautiful. All of us used to say that her mother must have given birth to her after eating a handful of pearls.'

The rain was falling hard now, big clear drops that exploded on impact into spider-like shapes. Azhar looked up at the sky drained of all colour. 'Yes, yes,' he said impatiently, 'but as I said, you'll have to talk to someone else.'

'She's an angel,' the man said, kissing lightly the tips of his fingers and letting them blossom in the air as though suggesting an aroma. 'Or, at least she was nineteen years ago.'

The number of years caught Azhar's attention. 'Does this have anything to do with those letters?' And without waiting for the answer he asked the man where he was from.

The stranger said he had come from one of the neighbouring towns and told Azhar how at the age of nineteen – some twenty years before – he had run away from home to become a film star. On reaching Lahore, the provincial capital and centre of the country's film industry then as now, he posed for a large portfolio of photographs which he financed by working as a labourer. In it he appeared in various get-ups: a sufi, a Chicago gangster, a she-rat hermit from Shah Dola's mausoleum, a Tarzan. Nothing, however, came of his fantasy: after being turned away by every film studio he went back home vowing never to make another journey to the cruel city. He kept the promise he had made himself for almost nineteen years; then, a fortnight ago – on becoming the recipient of one of the lost letters – he had gone back to Lahore. As a labourer he had lodged above a cheap wayside tea-house. The cook, a large woman who smoked constantly and used language more coarse than any man, had a daughter – an illegitimate child, many said, but no one had the courage to ask. The letter – a confession of love – was from this girl. A number of inquiries in Lahore had led the stranger to this town where, he believed, the girl – now, obviously, a grown woman – lived as someone's wife. A truck on its way to the North-West Frontier Province had agreed to carry him and had deposited him on the outskirts of the town in the early hours of the morning.

'I never knew she loved me,' he said. And showing his teeth again he reached into his pocket. '*It rains on my soul all night*. Would you like to read what she wrote?'

Azhar took a step backwards. 'No,' he said forcefully, repelled by the offer. 'You'll make trouble for whoever she is,' he said, and in a different tone he added: 'You should forget about the whole business and go back.'

To the stranger who had spent ten days travelling across the province the advice appeared insensitive. 'The roads are under water,' he said wearily, 'and there are no buses. I'll *have* to stay.'

'What about your own wife?' Azhar asked. 'Are you married?'

The man grinned. 'I have fourteen children.'

Azhar agreed to take him to one of the mosques.

Maulana Hafeez was getting ready to return home.

He received the traveller with a vigorous handshake and, learning that he had spent the night on the road, immediately set about improvising a bed in one of the more secluded corners of the hall. The traveller meanwhile set his suitcase in one of the alcoves – arched like the base of a flat-iron – and took out a set of dry clothes. When he went out to the baths Azhar too turned around to leave.

'Azhar,' Maulana Hafeez called as he finished making the bed. The word echoed in the space bounded by the empty walls and the high ceiling decorated with complex patterns of interlacing clubs, diamonds, spades and hearts.

'Yes, Maulana-ji.'

Maulana Hafeez approached and placed a hand on Azhar's shoulder, but remained silent – hesitating.

'Is it something important, Maulana-ji?' Azhar asked politely. 'It's just that I have a lot to do today.'

'It's nothing,' Maulana Hafeez said softly. 'It can wait. It can wait.' He patted the young man's shoulder and smiled. 'Go now. May God be with you.'

The song ended. The stylus crackled for a few seconds and then the singer spoke her name. The machine clicked off.

'Malika Pukhraj.' Alice repeated the singer's name as she entered the room. Mr Kasmi had just placed the small round mirror on the shelf. Alice had been waiting outside the bedroom for Mr Kasmi to finish clipping the tiny hairs on his cheekbones; somehow she knew that it would embarrass them both if he was seen to be doing this. 'Her daughter too is a singer now,' she said, 'Tahira Sayad.'

Mr Kasmi eased the little scissors off the knotted joints of his fingers. 'I didn't know Tahira Sayad was Malika Pukhraj's daughter.'

The girl nodded. Using a large goose wing she began to dust the surfaces in the room. Mr Kasmi crossed to the gramophone. For years he had lived with the handful of complimentary records that came with the machine, forcing himself to appreciate the songs which he would not have otherwise listened to. Then one day he found out that records could be bought separately – that a favourite song too could be owned. That very day he took a trip to Lahore and that night, even though shattered by the two-hundred-mile journey by arthritic buses, he stayed up late tapping his feet gently and shaking his head from side to side in time to melodies that were more in keeping with his romantic soul.

'It wasn't too loud, was it?' Mr Kasmi returned the record to its sleeve. 'There *has* been a death in town.' He inserted the record in its alphabetical place on the shelf.

Alice shook her head. She had picked up the cup of coffee – cold and more than half full. 'You didn't finish your drink.'

'It smells of turpentine. You must have forgotten to wash your hands properly.' Mr Kasmi had the taste of whitewash on his palate. Cautiously, Alice raised the cup to her nose. Mr Kasmi asked her where Zébun was.

The goose wing lay on the shelf. Alice had begun making the bed. 'She's downstairs in her room,' Alice answered from behind the billowing bedsheet, 'reading your people's holy book.'

Walking lightly on the balls of his stockinged feet Mr Kasmi came to get his shoes from under the bed. 'The Qur'an, girl,' he said as he stood up. And reasserted gently, 'The Qur'an.'

She smiled sweetly and shrugged. Her cheeks were smudged with cheap lali rouge, gaudy and bright. When she finished the bed she made a noise at the back of her throat to attract Mr Kasmi's attention, then straightened and with a playful gesture towards the clean sheet free of wrinkles and the elegantly arranged pillow said, 'Five extra marks for neatness, teacher-sahib?'

Mr Kasmi responded with a smile. He picked up his leather bag, collected the umbrella hanging from the wrought-iron S by the door and, crossing the small landing overlooking the courtyard, went towards the staircase. He descended the worn steps slowly, with both hands held gently against the wall. The steep flight of stairs had been crammed into one corner of the courtyard to give access to the top storey – Mr Kasmi's room, the landing, and a bathroom – which was added some time after the original house was built. At the bottom of the stairs Mr Kasmi paused as though getting used to the ground extending far beyond his feet.

The rain had thinned into drizzle, and there was a weak sun. A group of people – men, women and children – was on its way to the other side of the town where a goat had given birth last night to a kid on whose pale-brown hide the name of the Prophet appeared to be inscribed. The holy word – black and grey – was clearly discernible amongst the other markings. On turning the corner Mr Kasmi heard the clang of the butcher's cleaver. Zafri the butcher's shop was in one of the two rooms alongside the mosque. The shops were topped by a colonnaded balcony; the bubble-like dome above the main body of the mosque was out of sight but the tips of the two minarets could just be seen. Rent from these shops went towards the upkeep of the mosque.

On the raised platform outside his shop the barber stood leaning against the glass window. In the space below the platform were the open drains that originated in the mosque. During summer the shop would be resonant with the buzzing of the flies beneath the floor. On seeing Mr Kasmi, the barber went into the shop and began dusting the cumbersome chrome and leather chair: everyone in the town knew that Mr Kasmi used a shoehorn to ease his heels into shoes. Working the crank, the barber adjusted the head-rest to Mr Kasmi's level.

But Mr Kasmi did not come in. Raising a hand from the doorway, he said, 'I've only come to take a look at the newspaper. They say that the news of Judge Anwar's death has appeared in it today.' It was more a question than a statement.

The barber took a stool from under the shelf, wiped it clean, and offered it to Mr Kasmi. In the small wooden cubicle by the window someone was whistling while they took a shower.

'Gul-kalam is mentioned in it,' the barber said with a smile and handed the newspaper to Mr Kasmi. 'He's been going around all morning telling people that his name's in the paper.'

Mr Kasmi arranged the pages in order. The General had threatened the death penalty for any 'wayward' journalist who dared 'denigrate' his regime. A deaf and dumb boy had been found murdered; he had been raped repeatedly before being bludgeoned to death. The monsoon had caused floods in Bangladesh.

'Page three,' the barber told Mr Kasmi's reflection in the mirror.

'He left behind seven daughters,' said Mr Kasmi. 'What will the poor widow do?'

The barber was polishing the white tiles of the shelf. 'They say he was hoping that Azhar would marry the eldest,' he said without interrupting his work. Mr Kasmi did not make a reply – he had found the news item. The barber spoke again, 'But Azhar obviously has other plans. I had often wondered why a man of his rank would want to live in a town like this.'

Mr Kasmi looked up. 'The man has to live *some*where.'

The barber shook his head. 'We never saw the last deputy commissioner, did we? All we ever heard about *him* was that he'd been found face-down in a stream with stones in his stomach. But this one comes to visit the Alis a few times and then decides to stay for good. Now we know why.'

Mr Kasmi rattled the newspaper derisively. The barber, however, was adamant: 'He controls the whole district. He controls all branches of the local government, is in charge of the administration of revenue, and on top of that – and I know because I read the paper every day from cover to cover – he is the district magistrate. No, no, Kasmi-sahib, he should be living somewhere much grander than this.'

Suddenly the whistling from the cubicle stopped and the man inside swore loudly. 'The water's gone off.'

The barber looked at Mr Kasmi apologetically and thumped the cubicle door with his fist. 'Have some shame,' he shouted, 'we're practically inside the mosque.' Then shaking his head gravely he went to adjust the levers on the tank.

Mr Kasmi folded the newspaper. 'It's only a few lines,' he said, picking up his umbrella.

'No one wants to know about us,' the barber said. 'It's taken three days for the news to reach them, and even then they get some of the facts wrong.' He raised his eyebrows behind his tortoiseshell spectacles.

'Yes,' Mr Kasmi said. 'It says that they made off with fifteen thousand rupees' worth of gold jewellery.'

Maulana Hafeez appeared on the other side of the street. The optician had today set up his stall – complete with his transparent, jellyfish-like umbrella – on this side of town. Maulana Hafeez had finished talking with him and now stood facing the barber shop.

Mr Kasmi stopped cold.

Maulana Hafeez crossed the street diagonally and went into Zafri's shop next door. Only then did the barber dare to look at Mr Kasmi. He was wiping sweat from his brow and in turn fixed the barber with his steely gaze. 'You missed out one of the deputy commissioner's functions,' he said through a weak smile to conceal his nerves. 'He also controls the police.'

The barber remained at the window until Mr Kasmi, his usual somnambulist's tread leaving momentary footprints in the rainwater, disappeared around the corner. Then he waited for the customer inside the cubicle to finish before going next door to Zafri's shop.

Sitting on a straw mat, his legs folded under him, Zafri was talking – protesting about something, it seemed – to Maulana Hafeez. He wore a look of incredulity. On a thread around his neck was a thick brass talisman. All about the mat were large sections of sheep carcass, wrapped in muslin. There were knives of various widths and lengths and a cleaver; and there was a dried palm leaf to wave at flies. Yellow spheres of offal bobbed like buoys in a bucket of water by his elbow.

'I can barely keep up with the rent, Maulana-ji,' he said, his arms open wide. 'What makes you think I can afford luxuries like a television?'

The barber raised his arms and rested his hands on the beam above the door; smiling, he looked in.

'There's an antenna on the roof of your house,' Maulana Hafeez said in a low voice. He was sitting to Zafri's left, in the only chair in the room.

Zafri became exasperated. 'That is a perch for my pigeons.'

Maulana Hafeez remained motionless for a few moments, then he looked up. The barber dropped his arms and, entering the shop, handed Maulana Hafeez the rent for the barber shop.

Maulana Hafeez stood up. 'Pigeons are unclean, na-pak, creatures,' he said looking down at the beads of the rosary. 'Remember, earthly pleasures are easily achieved but are of scant worth to us. God is the ultimate truth.'

Zafri cleaned under his nails with the tip of a thin knife. The barber, not wishing to appear too eager to take the seat just vacated by the cleric, remained standing in the corner.

'Don't forget to call on Judge Anwar's widow,' Maulana Hafeez said as he went towards the door. Then, looking at the barber he explained: 'A goat each has to be sacrificed for the eight lives that were saved that night by the Almighty's wish. And the meat distributed to the poor.'

The barber took the chair when the maulana left. Zafri remained silent, faintly hostile, lips pursed tightly below his moustache. Finally he said, 'Maulana-ji is the kind of man who would look for a bone in a hard-on.' The barber smiled uneasily; he could think of nothing to say. He had often thought that Zafri's aggressive manner resulted from his being sanctioned to draw blood and tear flesh.

Above them a papiha came out of the rain, turning its body upright for a brief moment, its delicate claws held out. It alighted somewhere on the mosque balcony. Breathing in the smell of congealed blood and the fragrance of red roses left behind by Maulana Hafeez, the two men talked on for almost an hour without realising. When Zafri mentioned the goat with the special markings, the barber laughed and said that the day before his dog's urine had formed a shape like a map of the country; he wondered whether that had any significance.

Zafri gestured towards the unsold meat piled before him and said, 'If Mujeeb Ali ever decided to get rid of his Alsatians I wouldn't be able to make a living.'

'Not many people can afford luxuries like meat these days,' the barber said.

Zafri picked up the palm leaf and waved it around, causing a cloud of flies to rise from the muslin and float upwards. Then he rested his head against the wall and said, 'With my luck the only letter I'll get would be a demand for a long forgotten debt.'

The barber smiled. He pointed with the thumb at the mosque behind them and said, 'Have you had a visit from the wandering film star yet?'

Zafri opened his eyes. 'Did he show you those photographs of himself?' And he laughed out loud. 'All I can say is he could not have found a better guide than Azhar. He knows where to find a pretty girl.'

61

The expression on the barber's face became serious. 'Perhaps the girl will change her religion and they'll get married – Azhar and that girl of his.' And when Zafri shook his head scornfully, he added: 'He must love her. That's why he stays here. He doesn't even have an office here, has to drive out to work.'

'Love!' Zafri laughed in disbelief. '*Love!* You've watched too many films, my putar. Or have you been reading the women's page again? His sort doesn't love anyone. He'll suck her juice out and then go after someone else, the lucky soor.' And reaching under the muslin, Zafri took out a sheep's testicle and shook it like a little bell in front of the barber's face.

Laughter from Zafri and calls of apology followed the barber as he stamped out of the shop and made his way along the platform. Some years ago Mujeeb Ali's youngest brother Arshad, then in his late teens but already as large and as formidable as either of his brothers, had come into the barber shop and settling in the chair, his chin resting on his breastbone, had asked for a trim. While the barber worked in silence the youth had slept, snoring loudly. Twenty minutes later, at being woken he had stretched his arms and legs, opened his trousers and – ready to doze off again – had said, 'Now shave me off down here.'

Zafri, who had somehow found out about the incident, had never let the barber forget it.

It had rained continuously since early afternoon. After Isha – the last prayers – Maulana Hafeez locked up the mosque for the day and, mentally organising a sermon for next Friday, walked towards Mujeeb Ali's house. The rain rattled noisily on the umbrella whenever he emerged from under the streetside trees. The unusually small number of men who had come to the mosque for the day's dawn prayers had alarmed Maulana Hafeez. On realising that attendance had fallen steadily over the past few days – owing perhaps to the fears aroused by the judge's death, or perhaps to the rains – he decided that the time had arrived once more for him to remind the faithful of the maxim that nothing pleased the Almighty more than a fast observed during summer – when as many as seventeen hours might separate dusk from dawn – and a prayer offered during winter – a time when the water for ablution was ice cold and the warmth of the bed inviting.

Ten minutes later he was sitting with Nabila Ali in her large orderly kitchen sipping tea from a white porcelain cup. One of the servant girls had hooked up his umbrella in the veranda and his cap had been taken away from him for drying.

'My mother-in-law, may she rest in peace,' said Nabila, 'used to say that monsoon is too pretty a name for a season as messy as this.'

Maulana Hafeez blew on to the tea. After only a few seconds the rich milk in the tea had caused a thin skin to form on the surface and it shimmered in parallel wrinkles under his breath. 'I've come to collect Kalsum's boy's wages.'

'It's the first of the month today. I've been expecting you, Maulana-ji,' Nabila said, reaching forward from her chair and touching Maulana Hafeez's forearm, 'I have an important matter to discuss with you, Maulana-ji.'

The maulana became attentive; he nodded and set down the tea by his elbow.

Nabila said: 'Maulana-ji, you have to talk to Azhar.' And she let a few moments go by in awkward silence, searching Maulana Hafeez's face for some reaction until he gave a faint nod and, confident that she had been understood, she added, 'It's a disgrace. And in broad daylight too.'

Maulana Hafeez carefully considered his reply. 'The more exalted in rank we are the greater the responsibility resting on our shoulders to set an example to others.'

Nabila agreed. 'He's an educated man. We should be proud of him.'

'I *do* intend to talk to him because it is a very grave matter,' Maulana Hafeez said. 'It's too late to pay a visit now, but tomorrow' – he smiled – 'God willing.'

Nabila's eyes flamed. 'It's an outrage against public morals and religion. I have also asked Maulana Dawood to talk to him.'

Maulana Hafeez nodded at the mention of the other cleric. Nabila Ali, unlike her husband, did not belong to the sect represented by Maulana Hafeez. She belonged to Maulana Dawood's denomination. She followed pirs and mystics and made pilgrimages to various mausoleums across the country; she believed in touching the lattice-work grilles of burial chambers. She would take trips – sometimes travelling for days at a time – to tie a ribbon on the branch of a sacred tree, praying for a male child. Maulana Hafeez's sect held all this to be as contemptible as idol worship. Because it accepted public donations the other sect's mosques tended to be exuberantly decorated in marble and mother-of-pearl. The anniversaries of the deaths and births of various learned men of the sect were rich pageants: of multi-coloured lights, passionate all-night recitals and extravagant meals.

Maulana Hafeez, however, directed most of the mosque fund towards the poor. Nor did he believe in celebrating anniversaries: did not the Prophet choose to die on the same day of the year as he was born because he did not wish us to waste time celebrating his birthday and mourning the day of his death, so that we could concentrate instead on his teachings? One of the many other points of dispute between the two sects were the refrains *ya-Allah* and *ya-Muhammad*. Maulana Hafeez would argue, sometimes in the Friday sermon which was relayed to the whole town over the loudspeaker, that since the Prophet was a mortal – as he continually stressed throughout his life – it was not correct to presume to suggest that he was *present everywhere* like his creator Allah the Almighty, the All-Encompassing . . .

At this moment the cook came into the kitchen carrying a bucket of milk. The surface of the liquid was covered with dense white foam which moved as a single mass. Tiny droplets of milk were caught in the down on the woman's forearm.

'There is a traveller in the mosque tonight.' Maulana Hafeez spoke to his beads.

Nabila immediately turned to the cook and asked her to pack a meal. The woman duly tied the food in a large square of floral cloth and, going to the door, called out for one of the male servants. Maulana Hafeez instructed him to hand the meal to his wife since the mosque's front door was locked. After the food had been sent off the cook picked up the empty bucket and, memorising out loud the number of plates, bowls and spoons sent to the mosque, went out to finish the milking.

'I came for the dead boy's wages,' Maulana Hafeez said. He had finished the tea and set the empty cup upside down on the saucer.

At that moment the door opened and Nabila's youngest daughter entered. She carried the cage containing her pet parrot. The large bright-green bird sat on the perch nibbling contentedly at a green chilli which it held in its claw. With a smile and a wink, the child raised the cage on a level with the maulana's face and invited him to place a finger between the bars, to tempt the bird into biting it.

Maulana Hafeez recoiled, pressing his spine against the back of the chair. Nabila got up and took the cage from the girl's hand.

'That thing is unclean, na-pak, my dhi,' Maulana Hafeez, smiling now, told the little girl. Then turning towards Nabila he said, 'It has no place in such a pious household. And worse still, it eats with its feet.'

Nabila was carrying the bird out of the kitchen. 'You came about the driver's wages, Maulana-ji. I'll see where Mujeeb-ji is.'

Maulana Hafeez let the rosary slide down to the crook of his elbow and lightly stroked the girl's hair. 'Name two fruits mentioned in the Qur'an.'

Almost every child in town had been asked the question at one time or another. The girl climbed on to the cleric's knee. 'Olives and pomegranates.'

Maulana Hafeez lifted her to the floor. She was the youngest of five girls. The three girls immediately older than her were at the moment in the large room across the courtyard being given private tuition by Mr Kasmi. Commuting by car, they attended a school in the neighbouring town – the nearest one for girls. The eldest daughter was now married – to a senator's son – and lived by the sea in the former capital. Her wedding had been a magnificent and imposing occasion. To accommodate the guests many of the streets were taken over by colourful marquees which billowed in the noon winds and threatened to uproot the houses to which they were attached by thick ropes. So many flowers were brought in that for many days afterwards milk gave off a faint fragrance of roses and ishq-é-péchan. The bridegroom's procession entered the town accompanied by a downpour of newly minted coins. The bridal gown was of the finest contraband silk – to satisfy Nabila a bolt was made to pass through a little-finger ring – and was so densely embroidered that it was virtually impossible to tell the colour of the original fabric. The women, to this day, never forgot the careless manner in which the bride had lifted her skirt, scandalously exposing her legs, while descending the stairs of the family house. Maulana Hafeez had expressed disappointment at the enormous dowry, reminding Mujeeb Ali that the Prophet's dowry to his daughter was a grindstone, a waterskin, a mat and one or two other modest domestic items. He had also been distressed by the eating arrangements, demanding that a chair be provided since he did not wish to appear 'like a mule put out to graze in a pasture'; and had, despite being offered a knife and fork, insisted on eating with his fingers, refusing to eat with 'weapons' like an 'English-sahib'.

Nabila came back. 'Mujeeb Ali is in the big room, Maulana-ji,' she said; and as Maulana Hafeez walked past her she said wearily, 'Maulana-ji, you trouble yourself every month, when the money could easily be sent to the mosque. Why must you insist on adding to our sins?'

Maulana Hafeez crossed the plant-choked courtyard. Every movement that the wind caused in the leaves and branches was amplified many times in the play of shadows on the white walls. A fruit tree planted close to the edge of the courtyard had directed all its branches away from the nearby wall; it was almost

66

as though a normal tree had been sawn in half lengthwise and made to lean against the wall.

Mr Kasmi had left. And the girls too had disappeared into the house leaving behind their satchels and books. Mr Kasmi had helped the eldest girl with all the subjects that she studied at school, but the metric system had been introduced since then and he was unable to teach mathematics to these younger girls. At the other door, Mujeeb Ali appeared to be seeing someone off – Mr Kasmi, the maulana presumed. He turned to look in Maulana Hafeez's direction. Maulana Hafeez smiled in acknowledgement but Mujeeb Ali gave no sign of having seen him – he continued to stare straight ahead – and then deep in thought turned back to fasten the door.

The money was ready. 'You're a good man,' said Maulana Hafeez. 'If you hadn't continued with the wages I don't know what that poor woman would have done.' He pointed to the photographs on the wall. 'Your grandfather too was a good man. When he died the district's courts were shut for a whole month.' Two decades or so before independence Sher Bahadar Ali was made an honorary magistrate by the British. Some time in the previous century the British had also awarded large tracts of Crown land to the Alis; Mujeeb Ali's great-grandfather was awarded the title 'Khan-bahadar'. Their wealth had increased tenfold since then – mile upon mile of fishing rights, hundreds of acres of woodland, hundreds of acres of farmland. The family owned twelve towns. 'But he became a little forgetful near the end.' Maulana Hafeez smiled at a memory. 'He would walk out of the mosque with the cap still on his head, and would have to turn back halfway down the street to bring it back. But I suppose it happens to all of us. I myself find it very hard to remember things these days.'

Mujeeb Ali straightened a cushion on a chair and carried it over to sit by Maulana Hafeez. Below the tangle of the greying eyebrows his eyes were tired.

Maulana Hafeez went to speak, hesitated, and then said quietly, 'Was that the teacher just now?'

'No, Maulana-ji,' said Mujeeb Ali, 'that was the police inspector stopping by for a few minutes.'

Maulana Hafeez returned the rosary to his pocket while his other hand sought the arm-rest of the chair. 'Is anything wrong?'

'They've arrested Gul-kalam.'

Maulana Hafeez leaned back, shaking his head. 'God be merciful.'

'He was involved in Judge Anwar's murder. They paid him to guard the street for a few hours and also got the layout of the house from him.'

'They?'

'We're not sure yet,' Mujeeb Ali said. 'They're still working on him down at the barracks. Something to do with those letters, some mess from nineteen years ago.'

'But . . .' Maulana Hafeez said in a tremulous voice, frowning, '. . . but those letters haven't been delivered yet.'

'No, Maulana-ji, you don't understand. They came from Arrubakook, where the letters *have* been delivered.'

Maulana Hafeez tried to contain the confusion in his head. He said in a low voice, 'I'll read a few sparas for him tonight.'

Mujeeb Ali straightened. 'And tomorrow, Maulana-ji, you'll have to talk to the postmaster.'

Maulana Hafeez blinked. He was shaking his head at the news.

'I would talk to him myself but . . .' Mujeeb Ali broke off and gestured with his hands, feigning resignation.

Maulana Hafeez understood the unspoken request. He asked, 'What is it you want me to say to him?'

'Those letters, Maulana-ji,' Mujeeb Ali spoke as though to a little boy. 'They cannot be allowed to go unexamined now.'

Maulana Hafeez leaned back in the chair again. 'That's out of the question. That would amount to theft and betrayal. If something is entrusted to us in good faith—'

'But, Maulana-ji, it isn't as simple as that any more. We've already had a *death* because of them.'

Maulana Hafeez resisted. 'That was an isolated incident. If our conscience is clear then we have nothing to be alarmed about.

The Almighty, as acknowledgement of the obedience to which he is entitled, preserves from danger those he deems worthy. No, no, there's no need for worry, I'm certain.'

'Maulana-ji,' Mujeeb Ali said irritably, 'when the news gets out tomorrow, the two things are going to become so strongly linked in people's minds that in future the one is bound to lead to the other.'

Tightly gripping the ends of the arm-rests Maulana Hafeez tilted his head and considered. His breathing was calmer now. 'What will I say to him? It's a matter for the civil authorities. I don't think he has it within his powers to suppress the delivery.'

Mujeeb Ali shook his head. 'Nothing will be suppressed, Maulana-ji. The majority of them, perhaps all of them, will only be delayed. We'll examine each letter and withhold any that might result in the kind of crime that has already taken place.'

'Who is *we?*'

Mujeeb Ali shrugged. 'A group of people, responsible citizens, chosen by . . . chosen by yourself and Maulana Dawood.'

Maulana Hafeez closed his eyes. After a few moments he opened them and said, 'I'll see what can be done. But I can't guarantee anything.' His voice was muted and uncertain.

*Sunday*

—

Placing a foot diagonally on to the sheet of paper Zébun carefully drew around it with the fountain pen. The outline would serve as measurement for a new pair of slippers that Alice was to buy for her. It was Sunday and Alice would be journeying, with her parents and a group of friends, to the neighbouring town for the ten o'clock Mass. It was the nearest Christian church and cemetery; and since there was a bustling bazaar not too far from the church Alice was often asked to shop for commodities that were either too dear nearer home or altogether unavailable.

The outline and the pen lay beside her on the bed. She had begun untangling the ribbons woven into her hair when she heard footsteps on the veranda. She could tell by the shuffle that it was Mr Kasmi and reached for her stole.

'It's you, brother-ji,' she said as Mr Kasmi appeared in the door. 'I thought it was that girl.'

Mr Kasmi reminded her that it was Sunday, Alice's day off. He was dressed in his usual blue-grey trousers and white half-sleeved shirt. He had come downstairs to pay Zébun the rent. When Zébun explained that Alice had promised to stop by on her way to Mass, Mr Kasmi said that the trip must have been cancelled because of the rain that had been falling without a break since yesterday afternoon.

'In all the years I've known her she's never missed Mass,' Zébun said, drawing the ivory comb through the curtain of grey and silver hair. The stole covered the other half of the head. She held up before her a small mirror, its bright reflection dancing on the wall behind her. The circular spot darted up towards the ceiling as she set down the mirror on the counterpane to receive the money.

73

Mr Kasmi had got to know Zébun soon after his arrival in the town, where he had come to make inquiries about a teaching post that Yusuf Rao – his friend since university – had written to him about. He had spent the first few days as a guest at the lawyer's house, and after securing the job – he would be teaching all subjects – had asked around for a room he could rent. He was told about Zébun and the upstairs room she had recently added to her house. Mr Kasmi still remembered clearly that one of the first things he had noticed about Zébun was her great delicate beauty. Other more subtle characteristics – patterns that needed the passage of time to make themselves clear – had been revealed over the twenty-four years that had elapsed since then. An irreverent combination of strict religious practice and blind superstition gave structure to her day. She prayed five times daily, regularly recited the Qur'an, said her rosary and never failed to observe Ramadan. And she never threw away her old clothes, clippings from her nails, or her loose hair.

'You must ask Alice to put up the mosquito nettings tomorrow,' Mr Kasmi said, following Zébun with his gaze to the other side of the room.

She placed the money in a small trinket box carved with writhing vines and returned across the room. 'I too heard mosquitoes last night,' she said, taking up the mirror and comb once more. 'I'll get her to buy some fumigation coils from the bazaar.'

Mr Kasmi looked across the courtyard at the front door. 'I don't think she's coming.'

'She'll be here. A talkative person is always late. She must have stopped by to chat at someone's house.'

Mr Kasmi smiled at the exquisite logic of the comment. He nodded. 'By now the whole town should be humming with the news about the nightwatchman.'

'Gul-kalam?' Zébun said with a puzzled look. 'What about him?' She was carefully removing the fine silvery strands caught between the ivory teeth and winding them around her finger until the tangle resembled a miniature bird's nest.

While Mr Kasmi spoke – repeating what he had heard last night from various people on his way back from Mujeeb Ali's house – Zébun, listening intently, pulled the comb through her hair, giving tentative tugs whenever the flow was hampered by twists and knots.

'No wonder they were able to walk in like relatives,' she said when Mr Kasmi finished. 'They'd arranged everything so carefully beforehand.' And she asked: 'Why did *he* do it?'

Mr Kasmi gave a shrug. 'The obvious reason, sister-ji.'

She nodded. 'Riddles appear so simple once you know the answer.' During the last elections Gul-kalam's brother's wrists were broken on Judge Anwar's orders because he had painted a banner for the opposition. The bone setter's treatment had gone wrong and both arms had shrivelled right up to the elbows. The crippled man who had once made a living by painting houses and caravans and carts was now dependent on his brother. Zébun said, 'These people from the mountains never forget an insult.' She collected the tiny hummingbirds' nests from her lap and stood up. 'To us outsiders, all that seems such a long time ago.'

'You're right, sister-ji. It does seem a long time ago,' Mr Kasmi said from the door. 'But don't forget that that man was reminded of it every day.'

Reaching under the bed Zébun had pulled out a small cardboard box and was placing her hair inside. Once full, the box would be buried in the flowerbeds. She pushed the container back under the bed and stood up.

Mr Kasmi was watching. 'You're still doing that, sister-ji?'

Zébun gave a nod, her eyes downturned. 'You yourself have just finished telling me what hate can do to people, brother-ji,' she said. 'I know they'll use my hair to cast a spell on me, do something evil to me.'

After Mr Kasmi had gone, Zébun performed her ablutions and took down the Qur'an from the top of the wardrobe. 'Poor man,' she said under her breath. With a clarity that defied the passing of more than three decades, the image of Gul-kalam as a twenty-year-old, leaning against the doorframe of her bedroom, remained with Zébun. She was alone in the house: the man who had had the house built – intended as a family home – had abandoned her two days before they were to be married, having decided at the last minute that the honour of his family, stretching back decades, was more important to him than his love for her, a woman of the hira mundi, the diamond market. She had turned around from making the bed and seen Gul-kalam – then unknown to her – at the entrance to the bedroom with his gaze fixed on her. The young man was not under the influence of hemp as she first thought but had drunk half a bottle of turpentine. For the next twenty minutes both of them had stared at each other across a distance of two yards without moving from their positions. The silence rang in Zébun's ears like the noise of cicadas. The room became saturated with the metallic smell of turpentine. Then he turned around and – swaying and gently stumbling – crossed the courtyard into the street.

Zébun shook her head to dispel the memory and opened the holy book.

Rain seeped in, in regular pulses, through a crack in the roof and grew into triangular drops. Azhar had been watching the ceiling for several minutes, half asleep; now fully awake he yawned and sat up. In another cot set by the opposite wall a policeman was asleep in his underwear, using his clumsily folded uniform as a pillow. His brass whistle and beret lay beside him.

Azhar rested his feet heavily on the floor and looked around. The skull-faced barracks was a relatively recent building. Before it opened there had been no police in the town. Minor fights and scuffles were resolved by the intervention of elders; and the consequences – always bloody – of vendettas and feuds over matters of honour or land were dealt with in the cities. Politics itself had not touched the town fully until a few years before. There had been no adult franchise until the beginning of the last decade; and the five months of unrest that had forced the first ever ruler to resign had been confined to the cities. It was only when the country's third chief martial-law administrator sentenced to death his immediate predecessor – the only democratically elected prime minister since independence – that police stations began appearing everywhere, even in the remotest towns and villages.

Azhar opened the door by the sleeping man's feet and went into the lock-up. A damp, dark silence seemed trapped inside this part of the building. The cells received no natural light and a dense smell – of urine and of the monsoon – hung in the air. One cell was bare except for a bucket lying on its side and a length of iron cable undone into asterisks at either end. In the centre of the other cell Gul-kalam lay hunched, his knees drawn up to his chest. His head hair and moustache had been shaved off. Azhar stared at him through the bars, trying to locate the familiar face behind the newly transformed features. Gul-kalam had bled from his ears and nose and both corners of the mouth. An electric wire hung from the ceiling but there was no bulb. Azhar yawned deeply and, shooing away the flies, came back into the office.

'Where are the others?' Azhar kicked the leg of the cot.

The policeman awoke. The inspector had gone home during a let-up in the rain, and the other sergeant on duty was at the tea-stall across the street, eating breakfast.

'Were you working on him last night?' Azhar gestured towards the door to Gul-kalam.

The man nodded. He yawned and shook his hairy shoulders, dispelling sleep.

'You should learn to be less noisy,' said Azhar. 'I couldn't sleep for all that noise.'

The man smiled, revealing a gold incisor. 'Lying is a sin, deputy-sahib. You were snoring like a whirlwind. I could hear you clearly through the walls.'

Azhar went outside. The rain was stopping. There were tiny water lizards – slimy, sinewy or, depending on the light, glimmering and prismatic – in the mud. Standing with his legs wide apart Azhar urinated on to the tyre of the police van. It was just past midday and between the arches of the courthouse typists were setting up their tables and chairs, machines, letter-writing manuals and almanacs. Yusuf Rao was coming along the street to open his office, his game leg lending a graceful rhythm to his hurried trot. Behind the courthouse, above the roofs and the tops of trees, were the minarets of the two mosques holding up the drizzly sky.

'I don't snore,' Azhar said when he came back inside. He walked around the desk and settled in the swivel chair. Behind him there were three rifles and cartridge belts studded with rounds. The old desk sagged creakily to one side, legs diagonal, like a puppy resisting being dragged along by schoolboys.

'Nobody believes they snore,' the policeman said, smiling. He was still in his shorts and vest.

The second policeman came in bearing a tray with an earthenware teapot and a small heavy cup. There was a plate of kulchas and a boiled egg. He cleared a space on the desk by pushing aside the telephone and the folders and files, and set the breakfast before Azhar.

'So,' Azhar said to the policeman who had brought in the tray, 'what happened after I'd gone to sleep? What else did he say?'

The man shrugged. 'I too left soon after you did, deputy-sahib. I couldn't watch what these cannibals were doing.'

The remark was met with a smile from the policeman with the gold tooth. Still half dressed he was on his hands and knees mopping up water with an inadequately small piece of cloth. 'He has no balls,' he said over his shoulder.

The other policeman's lips were set in a half-smile. He shrugged: 'I'm a poet at heart really.' And he unbuttoned the top of his shirt and briskly revealed the left side of the chest. Scrawled across the dark skin, just above the nipple, was Wamaq Saleem's signature.

'When did you meet him?' Azhar asked, dislodging a crumb from between his teeth with his tongue.

'Years ago in Lahore. I was on duty the night he was transferred from the fort in Lahore to the Montgomery prison. In the van I asked him to autograph my heart and had it tattooed in the morning.'

78

Outside, the inspector jumped under the shelter of the portico and, turning around, shouted into the drizzle, 'Don't swing your hips, son. Walk like a man.'

The small boy at whom the remark was directed looked over his shoulder with frightened eyes, then hurriedly disappeared into a small side street behind the courthouse.

The inspector was shaking his head as he entered the office. 'He turned into a *lane*,' he said as though to himself, loudly. 'Lanes are for women. Men keep to the open streets and roads.' He had changed into a clean uniform and his raincoat was draped over his head. He hung it behind the door and carried a stool to his desk. He looked at Azhar and asked, 'What's the plan for today?'

Azhar poured himself another cup of tea and broke the second kulcha in half; sesame seeds from the first floated on the surface of the tea. 'We've informed all the stations. I'll go up to Arrubakook today.'

'What about Gul-kalam?'

'Get him cleaned up,' Azhar said, standing up. He dropped the piece of kulcha into the tea. 'I'm going home to change. I'll come back and sign a court order and take him with me. He'll have to be signed over to them.'

He had reached the outside steps when the inspector shouted after him, 'Maulana Hafeez has been asking around for you, DC.'

One of the policemen came running to the door but Azhar nodded without turning around; he raised a hand to indicate that he had heard, and said he would call at the mosque before going home.

The police inspector smiled at the two policemen. 'Any guesses, boys, as to why the maulana wants to see him?'

His subordinates grinned.

Suraya opened the casements on to the courtyard. There was no rain and a breeze stirred the few gaunt leaves left on the arbour revealing their paler undersides. The clouds had disappeared for the first time in two days and the whole house was in sunshine.

Back on the cot Suraya raised the needle to eye level and fed the licked end of the thread through the eye. She tied a knot at the other end and, after leaning towards the window to make sure which was the right side of the fabric, began to make careful stitches. Maulana Hafeez – sitting across from her, rotating the rosary – raised his eyes at the sound of footsteps. It was Kalsum.

She was bringing in a large brass plate on which were arranged, on a lining of hairy fig leaves, dark figs and some bruised apricots. She set the plate before Maulana Hafeez and joined her sister on the cot.

'From the trees in the courtyard?' Maulana Hafeez smiled. He reached into his pocket, his eyes hard with anxiety, and felt the compact roll of the three hundred-rupee notes. Hesitantly, he brought the money out and offered it to Kalsum. Suraya interrupted her sewing, needle raised in the air.

Kalsum looked down at her hands and said evenly, 'He would have been twenty-one this December.'

Maulana Hafeez had relaxed his shoulders. 'It's not up to us to question the Almighty's will.'

Kalsum pulled the edge of her stole down to her eyes. She turned to her sister and said, 'I knew something terrible was about to happen. The birds had gone quiet in their cages just as they do before a thunderstorm. And then I heard a flutter of Izrael's wings.'

Suraya made a clip in the fabric with the tip of the scissors. 'The lawyer seems convinced that it was Mujeeb Ali who put our boy up to that crime and then afterwards—'

Maulana Hafeez raised his hands in protest. 'There's no evidence for that. I've talked to Yusuf Rao about this before but it seems I'll just have to go and see him again.'

'No,' Kalsum shook her head. 'Mujeeb Ali is a good man. He still gives me this money. He knows that my boy was loyal to him and his family. He proved his loyalty by expressing his anger towards the family's political opponent.'

Suraya completed a stitch and lifted her narrow face towards her sister. 'I was only telling you what that political opponent himself said to me the other day.'

Kalsum continued shaking her head. 'I have never believed in rumours. When the boy's father-ji died everyone said that Dr Sharif had poisoned him, because his business was bad for the doctor's practice. Do you remember, Maulana-ji?'

Maulana Hafeez nodded.

'But I was with him when he died. It was a glistening blue viper that came out from under the grass. I saw it myself.'

Maulana Hafeez remembered Kalsum's husband, a herbalist. He was a short, handsome man who had had an easy laugh and whose habit of always wearing white clothes Maulana Hafeez had taken to be a sign of piety and a becalmed spirit. There is, he would say, for every ailment a plant which you must either take or abstain from. He had planted trees and creepers around their courtyard, along with pots of herbs and ferocious agaves. The first three months of every year would be lush with flowers; and during June there would be fruit by the bucketful from a Kashmiri cherry tree. It was he who had proposed the remedy of loquat leaves to Judge Anwar, and once a year he would send a large vat of loquat vinegar to the judge's house.

Maulana Hafeez stood up. 'It'll be Zuhr soon. I'd better be on my way.'

'You must take these with you, Maulana-ji.' Kalsum pointed at the fruit and got to her feet. 'Apricots are good for the bladder. I'll give you some honey, too.'

Maulana Hafeez smiled. 'One year, I remember, the dhrake tree produced so much pollen that the honey was *green*.'

Kalsum had taken the plate into the kitchen. 'The bees never really came back after they put up the electricity pole by the trees. They must be afraid of electricity,' she said from the kitchen. 'Anyway, Maulana-ji, there isn't anyone around these days to milk the hives.'

A smile of reminiscence came to Maulana Hafeez's face. 'I helped with the milking one year. And during the next ablutions, when I ran my fingers through my beard, I found two bees there. I suppose it proves that it pays to say your prayers five times a day.' He had sat down. He looked towards the kitchen and said, 'Your husband, may he rest in peace, loved his bees.' And to Suraya: 'He loved this town. He settled here against his brothers' wishes. His brothers wanted him to buy land. Why waste money on bricks, they said, when you have a family house in your own village?'

'I know, Maulana-sahib.' Suraya nodded from the cot. 'They're a backward lot. When Kalsum didn't conceive during the first year of marriage her mother-in-law wanted her to drink a eunuch's urine and do Allah knows what shameless things with someone's first-born son's faeces.'

Maulana Hafeez murmured, 'Superstition is sin.'

They remained quiet for a while. Maulana Hafeez leaned back into his chair. He made to reach into his pocket for the rosary but stopped and asked Suraya, 'When are you returning to Canada?'

Suraya answered without looking up, 'I'm not sure whether I'm going back, Maulana-sahib.'

Maulana Hafeez brightened. 'So, you're thinking of coming back to your own country. And your husband and son? When will they come?'

Suraya shook her head. 'Maulana-sahib, I've left my husband.'

Maulana Hafeez considered the reply for a few moments. '*You've* left your husband?'

Suraya remained silent.

The cleric said quietly, 'But you've left a family there.'

'I left a family here when I went.'

'But this is unheard of,' Maulana Hafeez said through a little laugh. 'A wife's place is with her husband.'

'Even if he marries again?'

Maulana Hafeez straightened, but Suraya had not finished speaking. 'He says a Muslim man is allowed four wives. He wants a Canadian divorce from me so he can marry again in that country. He says in the eyes of Allah we'd still be married since our Muslim marriage is not affected by the Canadian divorce.'

'Islam does not condone polygamy just for the sake of it,' Maulana Hafeez said defiantly. 'There are strict requirements which have to be met if a man is to marry more than once. There are guidelines to be followed.'

Suraya smiled. 'He promises to provide for me. But I won't do it. That's why I went to see Yusuf Rao, the lawyer, yesterday. He says he doesn't know much about Canadian laws but he's sure that in those countries a woman cannot be made to do such things. He's going to find out more about it.'

Maulana Hafeez was visibly shaken. 'There are conditions which have to be met before—'

Suraya interrupted him with a frown. 'But no one pays attention to those, do they, Maulana-sahib?'

Maulana Hafeez examined her face. Her skin was pale from the cold climate of the far-away country. She was much paler than anyone in this town where everyone had just spent several months under burning skies. And the skin on her hands seemed translucent, like the outer layer of puri-bread. She bit the thread between her teeth and examined her work. Maulana Hafeez quietly stroked the insides of his shoes with his toes.

On the raised platform outside the post office the postman was playing a game of draughts with a friend. He had a ball-point pen behind his ear. They squatted on either side of the grid drawn on the cement in charcoal and pulled greedily on their cigarettes. They were using tops of two different brands of soda bottles as counters. Despite the smoke from the cigarettes there was a cloud of winged insects above their heads; and from time to time one of them would clap his hands violently above his head, momentarily resembling a Hindu idol. When they saw Maulana Hafeez appear round the corner both men quickly stubbed their cigarettes across the grid, scattering the bottle tops; and straightening up, pretended to be chatting innocently. The cleric was walking towards the post office.

Across the street men were beginning to gather for the evening outside the laundryman's shop. They lounged on a broken-down rope cot and pulled on a freshly kindled hookah. The owner of the shop was arguing with someone; no doubt, Maulana Hafeez reflected, the argument was over a lost shirt.

Maulana Hafeez entered the post office. The postmaster and his wife sat behind the desk in the centre of the room, making envelopes. The postmaster folded each oblong piece of paper along identical lines and passed it to his wife who ran a deft finger dipped in flour paste over the edges. The woman was pregnant and breathed with difficulty.

She greeted the cleric, then shamefacedly covering her protruding belly went to the door at the back of the office; it gave on to the room where the couple lived.

Maulana Hafeez seated himself in the vacant chair. All around the office were calico bags and parcels and packets. Diagonal rays of the westering sun entered through the window. Set by the hatch through which customers were served was a small balance and several coin-sized weights. The floor was strewn with paper, like the fake rubbish created for a railway station on a film set. The telephone, one of the five sets in town and the only one in public use, was on the shelf by the window; the shelf also held the telegraphing equipment.

Maulana Hafeez looked around him uncomfortably and made a few noises at the back of his throat, as though unsure how to proceed. Then he said, 'I'm sure you've heard about Gul-kalam by now.'

The postmaster looked at him in surprise. But he seemed to recover, and said, 'Yes, Maulana-ji, I have heard.'

Maulana Hafeez, head bowed, became aware of the younger man looking at him carefully and some of his earlier awkwardness returned. Eventually however he said, 'I was talking to Mujeeb Ali and—'

'Forgive me, Maulana-ji,' the postmaster interrupted politely, 'but I think I know why you're here. Maulana Dawood too was around earlier. I'm afraid my answer is no.'

And for a while he stared at the table, lips tight; Maulana Hafeez's head remained bowed; neither spoke. Then Maulana Hafeez said, 'It will benefit the whole town if those letters were examined before being sent out. We must do whatever we can to prevent another tragedy.'

The postmaster smiled. 'It's not the whole town, Maulana-ji. It's just the rich people that seem worried. If Mujeeb Ali has sent you here, then does that mean he's confessing at least to the crimes he committed nineteen years ago?'

Maulana Hafeez touched his arm. 'You're being unreasonable and refusing to see reason simply because of your personal feelings towards Mujeeb Ali. And, from the little I know about these matters, those feelings are in any case ill-founded. Mujeeb had nothing to do with what happened to you during those elections. Everything was done on the orders of the old deputy commissioner.' And, after a pause, he added: 'You must understand that the Alis suffered just as much under the last government. Land was taken away from them and their mills were nationalised.'

'I'm not a child, Maulana-ji. I *know* who prevented me from filing my nomination paper. But I also know what Mujeeb Ali's henchmen did to the candidates of my party in other towns. I was lucky in a way that the deputy commissioner prevented me from submitting my application, otherwise your Mujeeb Ali would have had the same things done to me. I know how people were prevented from casting their votes here and how the polling agents were made to sign the rigged results at gunpoint.'

'All that was a long time ago,' Maulana Hafeez said quietly. 'The ideal memory is one which only retains others' good deeds while forgetting those of our own.'

The postmaster said, 'This martial law has been an answer to Mujeeb Ali's prayers. The expropriated lands were returned, and the mills. His brother *has* become a minister, and they even have a deputy commissioner of their choice.' He sank deep into the chair.

For several minutes no one spoke. Then Maulana Hafeez said, 'So, the answer is no? You are turning me away?'

The postmaster continued to look at Maulana Hafeez. The conversation had called up the memory of old disappointments. He became quiet and reflective. 'To be honest with you, Maulana-ji,' he said with a sigh, 'I think that had the Mazdoor-Kisan party come to power it would have been a great failure. It assumed that people are good, that they would want to share their money and possessions, that greed doesn't exist.'

Maulana Hafeez began to say something but the postmaster continued: 'In a way, Maulana-ji, what I believe in and what you preach are not that different from each other. Though you wouldn't agree with me here, of course. We both want to believe that people are basically good while the fact of the matter is that people are born selfish. It's being kind and generous that we have to *learn*.'

Maulana Hafeez shook his head. 'No. It's the other way round,' he said. 'You mustn't let such dark thoughts enter your head. Come to the mosque one of these days.'

Outside the streetlights were coming on one by one; and in the deep-blue patch of evening sky visible through the window birds were returning to their nests. Three blocks away Maulana Dawood began the call for evening prayers. Maulana Hafeez stood up. 'It'll be Magrib in twenty minutes. I must go.'

The postmaster switched on the light. And almost immediately there were moths in the room, manically circling the naked bulb.

Maulana Hafeez turned around at the door. 'Wouldn't you at least think about it? We've already had one death.' He seemed to be pleading. 'You're committing the sin of rebellion.'

The postmaster gave a small laugh, wheezing in almost silence.

Maulana Hafeez turned to leave. The postmaster watched him as he descended the three steps to street level. He came to the door and said, 'And, Maulana-ji, tell Mujeeb Ali that I don't have the letters yet. So there's no need to break into the post office tonight. The delivery isn't till Wednesday. They'll arrive either tomorrow or the day after.'

In Maulana Hafeez's absence two servant girls, their charges on their hips, had gone into the mosque. They had been to see the tree split by lightning the night before. One of the girls held both infants against her burgeoning breasts while her friend went to the toilet. Maulana Hafeez returned to find the girl standing in the centre of the courtyard.

Fear clouded her eyes when she saw the cleric. 'The baby has . . .' her voice trailed away. She nodded at her feet: there was a small puddle of urine.

'A child's,' Maulana Hafeez smiled.

The other girl emerged on to the courtyard, swinging her braids.

'Your baby has done something on the mosque floor,' her friend told her.

The second girl immediately rolled up her sleeves. 'We'll wash the floor, Maulana-ji,' she sang out.

Maulana Hafeez dropped his eyelids. 'You shouldn't be out at this time, kurio.' He pointed the crook of his index finger up at the darkening sky. A few of the nearer stars were becoming visible.

He sent the girls away and got ready to bathe the mosque floor.

The bricks released as steam the heat they had absorbed during the day. Maulana Hafeez held the earthenware ablution pot against his hip and with a twig broom in his other hand, swept the na-pak water towards the drains.

As he straightened from placing the pot and the broom by the row of ablution taps, Maulana Hafeez saw Mujeeb Ali standing in the doorway, removing his shoes to enter the mosque. He was accompanied by four men Maulana Hafeez did not recognise, two of whom were also removing their sandals. The other two were motionless, one on either side of the door, standing in the strip of unconsecrated floor. Over their shoulders the four strangers wore shotguns, barrels downward. Mujeeb Ali directed the two barefooted strangers to the hall and walked towards Maulana Hafeez.

Maulana Hafeez fumbled in his pocket for his glasses and watched the two men disappear into the hall. There were muffled sounds of a struggle from inside.

Mujeeb Ali shook Maulana Hafeez's hand and said something which the cleric did not catch – his gaze was fixed beyond Mujeeb Ali's shoulder on the entrance to the hall: one of the men had come to the door, carrying the traveller's suitcase tied shut with a rope and, with a nimble swing of the arm, he tossed it across the courtyard. It followed a shallow arc – its apex just short of the street door – and landed unopened out in the street.

'For God's love!' Maulana Hafeez extracted his hand from Mujeeb Ali's grip.

The traveller was being led out of the hall by the second man – one hand wrapped around his neck, the other gripping a forearm – and there was a violent jerk every time he resisted.

'Mujeeb,' Maulana Hafeez said, 'stop them.'

The man leading the traveller came to a halt, and glanced at Mujeeb Ali. A nod and he resumed walking, pushing the other towards the door.

'He's a guest in God's home. We have no right to treat him this way,' Maulana Hafeez protested.

'Forgive me, Maulana-ji,' Mujeeb Ali began at last, 'but do you know who that man is? Do you know what kind of questions he's been going around asking?'

'I thought he'd come to see that goat,' Maulana Hafeez said uncertainly. 'And even though I disapprove of such things I couldn't turn away a traveller. I was intending to talk to him about it soon.'

Once in the street the traveller was released. His shirt was torn at the neck and there were scratches on his throat.

Mujeeb Ali shook his head with a little smile at the cleric's reply, and explained the reason for the traveller's presence in the town. 'This is a decent town, Maulana-ji,' he concluded, 'for decent people. We don't want people like him roaming around amongst our daughters and sisters.'

Maulana Hafeez spent a few moments calming his breath. 'Anger is sin, Mujeeb,' he said and added, 'Get those guns out of the mosque.'

Mujeeb Ali waved the men out of the mosque and began to put on his shoes. Maulana Hafeez followed. When Mujeeb Ali stood up the cleric said: 'I went to see the postmaster earlier. He said that—'

'I know.' Mujeeb Ali raised his hand. 'Maulana Dawood went to see him this morning, Maulana-ji. I was on my way to the post office just now when I remembered about the wandering hero.' He smiled.

Maulana Hafeez glanced sharply at the four men standing outside the mosque. He grabbed Mujeeb Ali's arm. 'Mujeeb!'

'Don't worry, Maulana-ji.' Mujeeb Ali patted the cleric on the shoulder. 'Everything will be fine.' He pointed at the clock on the veranda and said, 'Shouldn't you be making the call for Magrib, Maulana-ji?'

※

*Once a day I have to walk to Bano's house for fire. Swinging the terra-cotta bowl of the hookah, I cross the street and enter the field. The air is hot and dry but the grass around my feet is damp. A band of gypsies sifts the rubbish dump, searching for bones to sell to the fertiliser factory. A grimy finger burrows deep into the filth and fishes out a three-angled bone resembling a shoemaker's last. A ghostly berry tree, studded with yellow berries, reaches out from the courtyard of Bano's house and keeps almost half the street in shadow. Waxy ants drop on to the passers-by. Occasionally, a stone, thrown by a boy to dislodge the berries, lands in the courtyard. Bano sighs and says, 'If you have a fruit tree in your courtyard you should expect stones.' I cross the shadow-speckled hush of noon and knock on the door.*

*In the partial darkness of the veranda Bano sits sieving wholemeal flour through a muslin hammock. She is so engrossed in the chore that flies drinking fluid from the corners of her eyes go unnoticed. Below the hammock is a large brass dish which catches the shower of plain flour, to be used for making pastry. She raises an eyebrow for emphasis and asks me whose daughter I am. The corners of her mouth are white with froth. She claps her hands – imitating the fluttering of a butterfly's wings – and sends a puff of flour into the air. She takes the hookah bowl and goes over to the clay stove where the cow-dung fuel burns. Some hookah smokers, like Father, seem to prefer the cow-dung fire to ordinary coals.*

*Bano cuts off the whiskers of her marmalade cat; she says the plague germs are carried on a cat's whiskers. The cat and the goslings live in harmony. The goslings' tiny melodious whistles turn to trumpet-like honks with age. They peck at the balls of wool as Bano loops the strands around her left hand and elbow. The cat sniffs the core of an apple. It shivers.*

*The top two squares of each window have jade underwater mirrors instead of glass. Some of the panes are cracked and throw feathery rainbows across the veranda at certain times of the afternoon. Izmayal, Bano's husband, with a skin as deeply pored as orange peel, is in the small room off the veranda. He lies on his side with one bent knee raised in the air – a three-angled shoemaker's last. He cocks a finger at me. He exists outside the domain of mundane happenings. His time is not commensurate with the rest of the world. Ripe with wisdom, cunning and self-knowledge; manly, abstemious and brave, he is alternately execrated and idolised by me. He fought in the Bangladeshi war, and now has no feet. We lost that war and when he came back everyone spat at him. An old woman struck him on the face. He knows the names for the winds at every point of the compass. He taught me the rhyme that helps me to remember the correct spelling of Mississippi. He says that four fledgling hummingbirds can fit into the bowl of a teaspoon, and that an adult hummingbird, once stripped of beak and feathers, is no larger than a bumble-bee. With effortless regality he feeds shiny pieces of knowledge to me. What is manifest to him is news to me. And yet I am afraid of approaching him; I listen to his stories from the door. I scratch behind my right ear with the first finger of my left hand.*

*Once I found Bano struggling with the cork of a large bottle. She started, stammered and, recovering, said it was a king-size Coca-Cola bottle, found nowhere else but Lahore. Had I never seen one before? Hadn't I ever been to Lahore? No? I should get my mother to take me.*

*Once every three months Izmayal drags a rope cot out into the courtyard and pores over the columns of premium-bond-winning numbers.*

*The crispy brittle bonds look like toy money. Izmayal arranges them like a hand of cards before him. Bano circles the cot, praying. Izmayal crouches on all fours – a bee on a flower – and tries to match the numbers. The cot creaks its protest. A shout escapes Izmayal when the first few numbers of a winning sequence raise his hopes and guide him along, only to mock him with the last digit of the sequence. An infinite variety of options reveal themselves to him during these first few seconds. His frustration is evident from the throbbing of his temples and the tightness of his jawline. He gathers the bonds and puts them away to ferment for another three months. How could one's happiness be reduced to the status of a number in a sequence, he seems to be asking himself. Crestfallen, he pulls himself across the courtyard and the veranda and goes back to his room.*

*One of Bano's cows has a pink udder. It is here that a bat once planted its fangs. The bats wander all over the body, their heat-sensors searching for the tissue richest in blood. Bano calls me over and directs the pink appendage at me. I open my mouth and a thin thread of milk enters my mouth, clear of my lips. She lets me feel the calf's head for the stumps of the emerging horns.*

*I stand in the door and Izmayal explains to me what a shooting star is. Halfway through the explanation I lift an exultant finger in the air: I know what he's talking about. The cleric's wife says that they are arrows of fire hurled by Allah against the evil djinn when they try to attain to the lower heavens to overhear the conversation of angels. Izmayal laughs, slightly short of breath and with echoes that seem to unfurl for ever. His lips ride up his yellow teeth. 'There's no Allah, girl.'*

# Monday

—

Maulana Hafeez's wife picked up the large green envelope from the shelf. Earlier in the morning, while Maulana Hafeez was still in the mosque, she had found the envelope lying inside the front door. It was addressed to her and had been dropped through the door sometime during the night. On the back, beneath the circular shellac seal was the name and address of the sender: the letter was written by Maulana Hafeez nineteen years ago, from Raiwind – the site of an annual conference of missionaries from all over the Islamic world.

Maulana Hafeez leaned his head against the back of his arm-chair and looked up. High up, a female spider was knitting her hammock. Maulana Hafeez removed his glasses. He smoothed the soft hairs of his beard and turned his head sideways to stare through the open door of the bedroom on to the courtyard. Bright light filled the house and Maulana Hafeez could sense the impending heat of the rising sun. The monsoon was continuing – now smooth and appeasable, now dramatic and capricious. There were colours on the washing line and a series of parallel bars of sunlight – filtered grainily through the screens – fringed the edge of the veranda.

He straightened when he saw his wife come out of her bedroom, her feet entangled in the bars of sunlight as she crossed the veranda.

'This came earlier, Maulana-ji.' She placed the letter in Maulana Hafeez's lap.

She went to the other side of the room to bring a chair over to her husband's side. Maulana Hafeez examined the letter with a furrowed brow. There was a blank moment as he realised what he held in his hands. 'But today's only Monday. These weren't due till Wednesday.'

The woman was settled before him. 'They have been delivered,' she said. 'They say Mujeeb Ali and his men beat up the postmaster last night. But he insisted that he didn't have them yet.'

'That's what he told me.'

'The postmaster and his wife are not in town, Maulana-ji. They must've delivered them during the night and fled.'

Maulana Hafeez lifted his strained features towards her. 'But where could they have run to? That woman was . . . with child.'

His wife did not respond. She watched the envelope keenly. Maulana Hafeez applied vertical thumbnails to the caked shellac and snapped the seal into two half-moons. Inside the official green envelope was the original letter and four photostated sheets explaining the unusual nature of the correspondence. The train crash was described at length; there was a poorly reproduced photograph of the derailed carriages. The text seemed to Maulana Hafeez to be written by an investigative journalist for the Friday supplement. He read all eight sides. His wife sat by him, placid and calm.

At last, Maulana Hafeez picked up the envelope which, he now knew, he must himself have sealed and addressed nineteen years before. Scrawled on the paper in blue water-based ink – it had faded to a grey – were his wife's name and the postal directions: the mosque's name, the number of the street, the letter of the English alphabet assigned to the block. Maulana Hafeez could not recall writing the letter but he recognised his handwriting. He opened the side of the envelope with careful pinches, releasing a faint smell that was familiar to him as the smell of the cupboard in the mosque where old and torn copies of the Qur'an were kept.

When he finished reading, Maulana Hafeez refolded the page along the two creases and returned it to its envelope; he then placed the small envelope and the explanatory literature inside the larger green envelope. Then, with heavy limbs and unsteady hands, he tore the whole thing up.

There was a mass of green, pale-yellow and white squares in his lap when he looked up at his wife. 'It was nothing,' he said quietly. He collected the torn paper in his hands and stretched out his arms towards her, as though making an offering.

She stood up and took the scraps – each tiny square scuffed at the edges – and went into the kitchen. She threw the paper on to the fire. The flames changed colour briefly and then returned to their original yellow.

Maulana Hafeez pointed up at the spider when she came back. 'This room needs a clean,' he said.

The woman returned the chair to its original position against the wall. She glanced up. The spider was still working. 'Not till the rains are over, Maulana-ji,' she said in her usual neutral tone. 'And you had better put on a vest, Maulana-ji. The rains are bad for you.'

Maulana Hafeez was massaging his scalp. He yawned. 'Do you remember what Atya used to say? Seasons and governments are at their most dangerous whilst changing.' He gave a little laugh.

She forced a smile. 'It seems true, Maulana-ji. We're still paying for the last elections.'

Maulana Hafeez nodded. He looked out of the room. A sparrow was perched on the brass tap, drinking water by reaching down and inserting its beak into the tarnished spout. 'Yes,' he said. 'I missed Gul-kalam's whistle last night.'

The barber opened the paned door of his shop and peered out into the eleven o'clock glare. The street was deserted; only the trees and their shadows stood on the verges. He closed the door and came back inside. He reached under the bench and from behind the cardboard boxes he took out his radio. Wiping the dust from the top of the radio set with his left sleeve he carried a chair to the electric socket. He put the radio on the chair, pushed home the two prongs of the plug and placed an eye to one of the holes punched into the back of the set: the glass valves were beginning to give off a saffron glow. The bakelite casing had three large cracks which had been mended with criss-crossing copper wire, like a stitched up wound, and a resinous substance resembling living eggwhite.

Once whilst sweeping the floor the barber had dragged the chair with the radio aside, forgetting that the set was still plugged in. It was pulled off the chair and hit the wall. The casing was broken but the circuits still received, enabling the barber and Zafri to continue listening to their favourite programme, while three walls away Maulana Hafeez slept his after-breakfast sleep.

While the radio was warming up, the barber went along the platform to Zafri's shop. To keep out flies and marauding cats the door to Zafri's shop had been pulled to. By the door a cloud of flies hovered above the large drum into which chickens were thrown to die after their throats had been cut. The drum was set at ground level and reached up to touch its rim against the platform. Its lumen was coated with blood, feathers and blue faecal matter. The dying bird would thrash about inside the drum, hurling itself against the sides, as though electric shocks were being applied to its little body. Sometimes a bird, squawking with fear and pain, would rise up to the top of the drum obliging Zafri to hurriedly improvise a lid.

The barber rapped his knuckles on the door and said, 'Time for Talkeen Shah.' He parted the door and poked his head in.

Zafri was wrapping a headless carcass in muslin. He hung it by the hind legs from the hook attached with a rope to the ceiling. The meat dangled – the amputated front legs a foot or so above the floor – in a posture which the live animal might have adopted when jumping over a fence. Zafri then locked the door and followed his friend into the barber shop.

'What happened in the last episode?' Zafri asked distractedly as he sprawled himself on the bench, using a towel as pillow. The barber checked the top of the radio for warmth. The programme, *Life and Opinions of Talkeen Shah*, was in its eleventh year. It chronicled twice weekly the wayward fortunes of the eponymous hero – an eccentric, unfailingly charming figure; middle-aged, and bitter at having been denied wealth and status. He had somehow – the account was altered regularly by him – fetched up in a leafy suburb of Lahore, where he now spent his days brooding over his unrequited love for the lady next door, a kindly college professor – and nostalgically looking back to the days before the Partition. And everything in life – the widespread corruption, the state of the young people, the high cost of living, the latest scandal from the film world, the smuggling and the kidnappings – everything was brilliantly lampooned as Talkeen Shah worked himself into impotent rages over minor incidents around the neighbourhood. The barber reminded both Zafri and himself of the previous episode. They laughed.

The radio was taking a long time to warm up. The barber anxiously consulted his wristwatch. 'My boy had better do well in his matriculation next June,' he said. 'Otherwise he goes straight to Saudi Arabia to work and send me a new radio.'

'We'll all have to leave for the Arab countries soon. There won't be any young men left in the country,' Zafri said, rearranging the pillow behind his head. 'Mansoor's brother is in Kuwait, earning fifteen thousand rupees a month. Mansoor orders meat almost every day now.'

'The boy was only sixteen when he left. He's just sent them a television and a camera.'

'I know.' Zafri smiled. 'Maulana Hafeez has been round to see them about it.'

The barber smiled. The radio came on, a ballad faded in. The barber lowered the volume.

'What annoys me is the way these maulanas never preach to the rich people. They're always asking *us* to come to the mosques,' Zafri said.

The barber settled in the large cuboid chair. He planted his feet against the wall under the shelf where grime deposited originally by customers' feet was now in the process of being eroded by those same feet; the original colour of the paint showed up, gleaming. He said, 'They forget the sura which says' – and he quoted in Arabic – 'he who amasses riches and scandalously hoards them, thinking his wealth will render him immortal, he shall be flung into the Destroying Flame.'

Zafri waved away a fly and yawned as the barber translated the verses. When the barber finished Zafri said, 'Look what happened at the post office last night. But neither of those two will talk to Mujeeb Ali about it.'

The barber smiled. 'But didn't the postmaster retaliate in style!'

Zafri grinned with relish, slapping his thigh with the flat of his hand. 'Right under the noses of Mujeeb Ali's men who were patrolling the streets.' And he added: 'I myself would have gone one step further. I would have written some letters myself, one to each person in town, listing the crimes the rich have committed against us since the beginning of time.' He was beating out the rhythm of the ballad on the bench with his fingernails.

The barber laughed loudly. 'That would be called the opposition press, and would either be censored or banned altogether. So, my putar, we'd be back where we started.'

The announcer was reading out the names of the people who had requested the ballad just finished.

'I wonder where they've run to,' Zafri said and asked, 'Who's taking care of the post office today?'

The barber was following the new song with his eyes shut; the male singer whistled between lines. 'Mujeeb Ali has posted two of his goondas outside the door.'

'I really didn't think anyone had cause to worry. What could a letter possibly contain? News about Auntie Nasima's bunions, little Nani's milk-tooth.'

The barber agreed with a nod of the head, while at the other end his feet kept time to the furious beat of the song. 'Nothing has happened so far,' he scoffed, 'and they have been in people's possession for ten hours at least.'

A faint layer of crackle developed in the reception. The chirpy song was beginning to disappear behind interference. The barber got up and altered the position of the set a few times until the reception improved, then he reiterated his intentions concerning his son's future.

Fifteen or so minutes later, when both of them had become absorbed in the broadcast, a car drew up outside. It was a cool blue in colour. On the front door, along the length of its chromium strip, the sun was reflected in two glaring shrapnel points which merged, and then vanished, as the door was opened. The tired-looking man at the wheel got out. The passenger seat was empty but someone was stretched out in the back of the car, dozing. The driver looked about him for a few minutes. His ruffled hair and clothes told of a long journey. A broad triangle of damp pointed along the line of his spine and there were creases behind the knees on the trousers. He walked up to the barber shop and tapped with a fingernail three and a half times on the glass.

'We're looking for Yusuf Rao's house,' the man said on being invited inside. 'He's a lawyer.'

Zafri sat up with an irritated look: the barber was turning down the volume. The newspaper Zafri had been lying on – now corrugated from being pressed into the slats of the bench – drew the stranger's attention. 'I see you buy the newspaper I work for,' he said. There was a pile of newspapers under the bench waiting for Zafri to carry them to his shop.

'Are you a journalist?' the barber asked, a little awed.

The stranger shook his head. 'No. I'm just a photographer.' He gave his name and pointed through the window at the car and said, '*He*'s a journalist.' The man in the back seat was getting out of the car. His face, too, showed signs of fatigue.

'We have come to cover the story of the lost letters,' the photographer said. 'I believe they're being delivered on Wednesday.'

Zafri and the barber looked at each other.

The journalist came into the shop. 'Saif Aziz,' he introduced himself – with the city-dweller's characteristic directness – and shook hands with Zafri and the barber. He moved to the centre of the room directly below the ceiling fan, and opened his shirt. From there, his eyes closed, he asked for some water.

The barber had been reaching under the shelf. He pulled out a large thermos flask. The inside, lined with emerald-like glass, contained lozenges of ice and also the barber's lunch: two mangoes. The fruit was streaked with dried juice which retained the imprint, back to front and upside down, of the newspaper it had been wrapped in.

Saif Aziz drank the iced water deeply. He appeared to revive.

'Are you friends of his?' Zafri inquired politely. 'Yusuf Rao's?'

Saif Aziz nodded. 'Since law school,' he said. 'I failed my exams and had to do this' – he wrote with an invisible pen on the palm of his left hand – 'for a living.'

Both Zafri and the barber nodded. The barber was about to speak when the photographer seemed to notice the radio in the background. 'Ah,' he exclaimed, 'you were listening to Talkeen Shah.' He walked over to the radio set and turned up the volume.

'Poor Rukaya is dead,' Saif Aziz said. Rukaya was Talkeen Shah's secret love, the woman he longed for.

The barber looked up. 'No, *no*. She has gone to live in England. She is not *dead*.'

Saif Aziz's face was beginning to lose its red glow. He ran his fingers through his hair. 'The actress who was the voice of Rukaya has died,' he explained. 'So the scriptwriters were forced to send her abroad.'

Both Zafri and the barber wore baffled expressions. 'Dead?' Zafri said in a low voice. 'But she writes regularly. Talkeen Shah waits for her letters. He fights with the postman whenever a letter is overdue.'

Saif Aziz and the photographer seemed amused by this confusion. The photographer shrugged.

Then the barber stood up. 'There is something you should know about those lost letters.'

But Saif Aziz waved him down. 'I know about the judge's murder,' he said. 'Ours was the only newspaper that ran the story.' And he added in mock disappointment: 'Don't tell me you didn't see it?'

'We did see it,' Zafri said. 'But there's something else you should know.'

And the barber cleared his throat noisily before beginning.

Azhar's favourite dish was a kind of soup made by boiling for eight to ten hours sheep's hooves and shinbones. The cuticle of the hooves and the hairs on the skin were first singed over naked flame and scraped off. Then the hide was scored and the cuts were spiced. As the soup simmered, gelatin from the tendons was slowly released through the pores. The dish was served with opaque globules of gelatin and small pieces of bones like knotted branches floating on the surface, and was eaten with tandoori bread. Halfway through the meal Azhar would test how successful the soup was by pressing the tips of his fingers together. If the fingers stuck he would proclaim the dish a triumph: the soup had simmered long enough to allow the right amount of gelatin and marrow to ooze out of the bones.

Azhar had developed a taste for the dish during his student days in Lahore. 'I agree with Imran Khan,' he had often said, 'the best food in the world is sold on the footpaths of Lahore.' And the best in Lahore, according to Azhar, were the stalls in the hira mundi – that crimson lily floating in the dark waters of the Punjabi nights. No one doubted him: it could easily be believed that pimps and nykas, men and women whose business it was to gratify every desire, would only allow the best cooks to populate their streets.

Elizabeth gathered up her hair clear of her shoulders, leaving her earlobes visible, and secured it with two twists of a rubberband. She unwrapped the five trotters tied with coarse twine and lifted them to her nose to check for freshness. The smell was that of a recent wound. Satisfied, she cut the twine and placed the bony stumps widely spaced on the grill. She lit the fire underneath. The hairs curled and were gone instantly. The stench of burnt hair saturated the small kitchen. Elizabeth held her breath and prodded the stumpy bones with the knife.

Standing outside on the portico, about to knock, Mujeeb Ali too was overwhelmed by the smell of burning protein, dense and cloying. He frowned and knocked. Elizabeth turned off the fire, put the knife on the table with the other hand, and cast around for her slippers.

When she opened the door, Mujeeb Ali pushed her aside and stepped into the house. He crossed the courtyard with an even stride; only on reaching the veranda out of the echoing sun, did he turn around.

'Where's Azhar?'

The reply, too, was not immediate. Elizabeth pulled the door shut but did not fasten the bolt. 'He's out of town,' she said, glancing up at Mujeeb Ali as she came in out of the disabling heat.

'But the car is parked outside.'

Elizabeth cleared her throat softly. She explained that Azhar had taken Gul-kalam to Arrubakook in the police van.

Mujeeb Ali nodded. He stood a couple of paces to Elizabeth's left – set beside her slender form he seemed a colossus. He examined her openly from head to foot and said, 'Are you the maid?'

There was no reply. Instead Elizabeth briefly held Mujeeb Ali's gaze. Then she averted her eyes.

'No,' he answered himself. 'Of course you aren't.' No emotion seemed to inform his voice. Nor did his face register any expression. After a brief pause he said, 'Don't you have a stole?' He was pointing at her head, indicating that she was bare-headed before a male stranger.

She went to the back of the veranda and took down her stole from the hook. It was the same green colour as the chenille of her shirt. She draped it across her shoulders, her head still defiantly bare. Her features were rigid.

'Would you like a cup of tea?' she asked.

'No.'

'Don't worry,' she smiled, 'you'll be served in the cup out of which the Muslims of the house drink.'

'Watch what you're saying, girl,' Mujeeb Ali said sharply. 'I don't drink tea at this hour, that's all. Anything else has nothing to do with it.' And after a pause he added: 'My servants eat out of the same plates as me and my children. Only the people who come in to clean the gutters and unblock the drains have their things kept separate. But that's because they go down into filth, not because they're Christians.'

'I know,' said Elizabeth. 'My father cleans sewers.'

Their glances disengaged. Mujeeb Ali took out a handkerchief and dabbed his eyes, his skin shone with sweat. 'And what does your father think of *this*?' he asked without looking at Elizabeth. He had pointed at Elizabeth's clothes drying on the washing line.

There was a silence.

Mujeeb Ali returned the handkerchief to his pocket. 'You should convert and get him to marry you.'

Elizabeth looked up. 'I'd do it if Azhar asked me.' She spoke firmly. 'I won't do it so that others can sleep easy at night.'

Mujeeb Ali nodded slowly. He made a noise at the back of his throat and, becoming aware of the burnt hair once more, expelled the air from his lungs. He said, and this time he spoke politely, 'Tell Azhar that I called. Ask him to come and see me when he returns.'

Elizabeth too softened her voice. 'He's returning late at night,' she said. 'It will have to be tomorrow.'

The sun was entering the second half of its arc. Mujeeb Ali walked past the shut-up houses sleeping their siestas, past the straggly lime hedges.

As he neared his own house he saw Maulana Hafeez in the distance. The cleric was raising his hand and hurrying towards him. He came up close and they shook hands.

Maulana Hafeez let himself be ushered into the shade of a talli growing by the edge of the street and closed his umbrella, the canopy collapsing like a fleeing jellyfish. 'I have just been told about the postmaster . . .' He left the sentence unfinished, accusingly.

'Forgive me, Maulana-ji, but those letters had to be looked at. We agreed about that on Saturday night. He said he didn't have them but I knew that he was lying. And I was right.'

Maulana Hafeez said, 'But you promised me. And that poor woman . . .' Mujeeb Ali started to speak but Maulana Hafeez placed a hand on his forearm. 'I must have your assurance that if he does come back you won't harm him.' There was lunch on his breath and the skin around his eyes was still taut from his recent sleep.

Mujeeb Ali nodded half-heartedly and dabbed at his brow.

'It *is* hot,' Maulana Hafeez said. 'But I had to come and find you. Nabila said you weren't in.'

'I didn't mean to trouble you, Maulana-ji. But I was round at the deputy commissioner's house.'

Maulana Hafeez moved his hand to Mujeeb Ali's shoulder. 'I've been looking for him since yesterday. Is he back?'

Mujeeb Ali shook his head.

Maulana Hafeez released him. He lowered his head, looking at his shoes: on each foot the joint of the second toe peeped out of the hole made in the leather. 'I think you should talk to him, Mujeeb,' he said quietly. 'Get him to . . . mend his ways.'

Mujeeb Ali did not respond. He inhaled the attar gently released from Maulana Hafeez's clothes by the heat.

'Yes.' Maulana Hafeez spoke as though Mujeeb Ali had replied. 'He should mend his ways. He's an educated man. He should make us see that education doesn't mean you forget the difference between heresy and faith.'

Mujeeb Ali was edging towards the rim of the talli's shadow. 'We'll see what can be done, Maulana-ji.'

The cleric felt for the catch on the umbrella. 'And do you know what would make me really happy? If both of you were to find time to come to the mosque one of these days. Then I'd be able to hold my head up in the street. I know you're busy people but . . .'

Mujeeb Ali had given a little nod and was walking away.

Maulana Hafeez, his umbrella unfurled, watched him until he disappeared into the great marble house that dominated one side of the street. Then, ordering his thoughts, he began walking slowly back towards the mosque.

The boy set the four cups of coffee on the tray and, boldly balancing the tray on his splayed left hand, began to cross the street. The doors and windows of the courthouse were shut, only an occasional figure was to be seen wandering among the empty arches. The typists dozed in their chairs, wrists dangling near the ground. A herd of water buffaloes had come to rest under the trees on the river embankment. The beasts stood motionless, muzzle to flank, transfixed by the great heat. The boy went into Yusuf Rao's office. Ignoring both Yusuf Rao and Mr Kasmi, who was visiting, he made a slight bow towards the two men he had earlier seen arrive by car. He transferred the cups on to the table. Then he gathered up the lunch dishes and quietly withdrew. Outside he lingered around the car, touching the creamy paint-work and examining the tyres and peering through the windows, until his father's shout from across the street pulled him away.

Yusuf Rao began to hand round the coffee. The cups and saucers had chipped edges revealing the darker clay beneath the white glaze.

Saif Aziz took a small mouthful, cautiously. 'Where did you get coffee from?'

'A woman returning from Canada made me a gift of it,' Yusuf Rao said over his shoulder. And to Mr Kasmi he said: 'She came to see me as well the day before yesterday.'

Mr Kasmi, his fingers delicately curved, took the cup being offered. 'She's the aunt of the boy who fired the shot at Yusuf,' he turned towards the newcomers and explained.

The photographer sat on a stool by the filing cabinet, flicking through a magazine. Yusuf Rao set a cup for him on the shelf by his elbow and returned to his chair.

'Those elections!' Saif Aziz shook his head. 'How wrong you were, Yusuf.' He was frowning. 'You should have joined the Mazdoor-Kisan party from the beginning. I wrote telling you to do so. Instead you went around supporting their suppression.'

'Look, Saif, yaar,' Yusuf Rao said. 'I have *admitted* to being wrong in the past. I believed all the promises. I *believed* that the enemy wasn't just the rich and the powerful but also the dissident voices within our own party who criticised us for not doing enough. We thought that they would jeopardise the prime minister's re-election.'

'If more people had joined us from the outset then the country wouldn't be the mess that it is now,' Saif Aziz said. 'Now we've got this general who looks as if he won't budge without the help of dynamite.'

'But I wasn't the only one. Everyone was taken in by the lies,' Yusuf Rao said, but the conviction had gone out of his voice. 'I had the support of the whole town. Women didn't talk to Kalsum for months after her son fired that shot at me. And that poor boy himself . . . We all know how much his trying to kill me enraged the people. They beat him to death, on the spot.'

Mr Kasmi had been listening intently. He nodded, then said: 'So, Yusuf, you accept that it was not Mujeeb Ali who had the boy killed, that it was the people themselves who beat the boy out of loyalty to you.'

'No.' Yusuf Rao shook his head uneasily. 'It wouldn't have gone beyond a beating. After all, he missed. I have no doubt that there were people planted in that crowd who made sure that the blows did not stop until the boy was – well, dead.'

There was a silence.

Then the photographer exclaimed: 'Here's one of my photographs.' He folded the magazine on itself and offered it at arm's length to the others.

It passed from hand to hand. 'The only reason this magazine continues to publish is that it is in English,' said Saif Aziz. 'You couldn't get away with saying half these things in Urdu. They would have banned it years ago.' Saif Aziz's own name appeared on the back page, in the list of regular contributors. It was a name associated with numerous organisations that existed, to all intents and purposes, on letterheads only. He had also been thanked in the preface of a book published in England a decade or so ago. The author, an expatriate, had predicted with great timeliness the breakup of the country. But that was a long time ago: the book was probably out of print by now and the library copies would have been withdrawn and sold off cheap.

Two small boys dressed in soiled clothes appeared at the door of the office. Each carried high on his back a bundle of books. One of them stayed framed in the door, as the other entered the room and advanced towards Yusuf Rao's desk. On this he placed two rectangles of pink card. They were bus passes. Then the boy addressed Yusuf Rao, the man behind the desk: 'Can you put a rubber stamp on these, chacha-ji.' His voice was weak, melodious. He seemed to be standing to attention.

Yusuf Rao examined the cards. They folded like wallets. 'They should be stamped by someone at the bus station,' he told the boy.

But the boy shook his head. '*They* say they should be stamped by the post office but the post office is closed today.'

The second boy entered the office. He had been admiring Saif Aziz's car. 'They won't be of much use anyway,' he said. He seemed a little more confident, more expansive, than his friend. 'The conductors recognise us standing by the road and don't thump on the side of the bus to tell the driver to stop. They know we are free bus-passers.'

The first boy nodded his agreement vigorously. 'Then if we walk from our village we are late for school and the teachers punish us. And if we go back home our fathers beat us saying we missed the bus on purpose.'

The photographer watched the boys with interest. 'So what do you do?'

Both boys laughed noisily. 'We go for swims in the rivers.'

Yusuf Rao smiled and shook his head, then reached into the bottom drawer of his desk and took out an old rubber stamp. The rubber had become brittle and was flaking away, and many of the letters had crumbled. He flicked open the ink pad. 'I'll put one of mine on. The conductor won't know the difference,' he said confidently. 'He just needs to see a stamp.'

Once their passes were stamped the boys wheeled round happily and were gone.

Mr Kasmi shook his head and smiled. 'When I was their age my mother-ji would send me to the village blacksmith's shop every day. Sit and watch what he does, she would say, you'll learn something.'

The photographer's lips parted in amusement. '*My* mother would order me to stand by the mechanic every time he came round to fix something. And she used exactly the same words. You'll learn something.'

'Are you from one of the villages around here, Kasmi-sahib?' Saif Aziz asked. He was still examining the magazine.

Mr Kasmi looked at Yusuf Rao who said: 'No.'

The forcefulness of his reply, followed now by silence, drew the newcomers' attention.

'I'm from one of the villages that were burnt down under the last government,' Mr Kasmi said in a flat voice.

Saif Aziz rounded his mouth and shifted in his chair. 'You're an Ahmadiya, Kasmi-sahib?' The Ahmadiyas belonged to a sect considered heretical by purists. It was outlawed by the previous prime minister in an effort to placate the maulanas and to win over the religious vote.

'Do people know?' the photographer whispered urgently.

Yusuf Rao folded his arms in his lap. 'All the Ahmadiyas were driven out of the town and their houses razed to the ground. But Kasmi has never really been religious, so no one really knew. Everyone just loves and respects him as the man who pulled a generation's ears out of shape.'

The remark forced the others to offer awkward smiles. But the pretence at light-heartedness was short-lived.

Mr Kasmi stood up with a sigh. The sun was beginning to withdraw its rays. 'I'd better be getting back,' he said. 'Sister-ji will be wondering.'

Yusuf Rao swayed over to the door and shouted for the tea-stall boy.

Saif Aziz slapped his knees and stood. 'Tomorrow,' he said, 'we get down to business. Talking to the sixty-seven people who have received the letters.'

Yusuf Rao clapped a hand to his forehead. 'How could I forget,' he said. '*I* received a letter this morning. Or to be precise, my wife did.'

'What was it?' Mr Kasmi asked. He took down the umbrella from the hook and picked up the leather bag from the shelf.

'It was a letter I wrote to her from Lahore. I was away taking the bar examinations,' Yusuf Rao was laughing. 'She says I should be ashamed for writing such vulgar things in a letter. But I tell her that a man can write whatever he wants in a letter to his wife, especially a young man. She says didn't I know that the letter would be going into a house full of children – what if it had fallen into their hands?'

'Well, that cuts down our work.' Saif Aziz nodded at the photographer and grinned. 'Now we only need to talk to sixty-six people.'

*Tuesday*

—

By the time Zafri slaughtered the seventh goat a crowd of beggars had gathered outside Judge Anwar's house. Indifferent to the rain, beggars of all ages – from very young to extremely old – jostled and fought each other to reach the front door. One seemingly able-bodied man wore a framed statement around his neck that carried his picture and proclaimed him deaf, dumb and blind. Azhar and Dr Sharif made their way into the house with difficulty. A blind woman – irises flickering for lack of anything to focus on – cursed loudly when Azhar pushed her aside. She was accompanied by a young girl who had tangled hair and clogged nostrils. The old woman's left hand rested on the girl's right shoulder.

'This isn't the granddaughter you had with you last week,' Azhar shouted over his shoulder as he crossed the rainy courtyard.

The woman recognised the deputy commissioner. 'The other one is getting old, deputy-sahib.' She turned her blind eyes towards Azhar and shouted out her reply. 'I can't drag her around for every Ayra, Gyra and Natho-khyra to lay eyes on.'

Plants had been taken down from the eaves. Instead, from the hooks hung the disembowelled carcasses of the seven goats. The black-and-white checked floor of the veranda was wet with orange, watered-down blood and fluids the colour and consistency of melted butter. The pots of ferns were set against the back wall, and next to them in a neat row were the heads of the sacrificed goats. Their small eyes were like marbles. The long, velvet-encased ears rested softly on the tiles like robes. The ribbed horns curved backwards and touched the wall.

Despite the rain both Dr Sharif and Azhar hesitated before stepping on to the veranda. The young boy assisting Zafri was dragging the eighth goat on to the veranda by the rope around its neck. The animal, sensing the danger, struggled and bleated. Zafri held the

knife between his teeth and, with a quick movement of his right
foot across the goat's front legs, threw the animal to the floor. His
movements from then on were perfectly co-ordinated; the actions
of the assistant, however, as he grappled with the writhing rump
and hind legs, were haphazard and betrayed his lack of experience. Once the animal was overpowered, the boy shouted for
Asgri Anwar.

Asgri emerged from the room adjoining the veranda – the
room where Judge Anwar was killed. She carried her youngest
daughter on her hip. It was necessary for the person in whose
name the sacrifice was being made to touch the knife. Zafri
raised his head, the blade between his teeth, and the little girl
reached down to touch the wooden handle.

Zafri took the knife from his mouth and – his lips moving as
he read the appropriate verses – opened the animal's throat with
short, precise cuts. Azhar watched for a few moments then
looked away. Buzzards and kites and vultures floated above the
house. Crows topped the outside walls, evenly spaced as though
arranged there by a human hand.

'So how's my friend Gul-kalam, deputy-sahib?'

A few moments passed before Azhar realised that Zafri had
addressed him. Asgri, on her way back to the room, stopped and
looked back at the butcher. He was concentrating on the blood
gushing out of the opening in the throat, his knees pinning the
dying animal to the floor. The blood poured out with great force:
it was almost as though it was this force, and not the knife, that
had torn open the blood vessel.

Dr Sharif said under his breath, 'Death may be an important
part of nature but there's nothing more unnatural than a dying
animal.'

The boy let go of the hind legs. The animal had stopped trying to kick. And within the next minute an eighth head joined
the other seven by the wall. Dr Sharif noticed that one of Zafri's
fingers was bandaged. He remarked on it.

'I cut it on a bone,' Zafri explained. 'Now I understand why
the cave people used to make weapons out of bones.'

Dr Sharif advised him to stop by at the surgery later. 'Wounds don't heal well in the rainy season. Damp, you see. Risk of infection.'

Zafri smiled. 'You're not going to pick my pocket that easily, doctor-sahib.' He gave his eyes an upward roll. 'I'll just piss on the cut and cover it with burnt cloth. It'll be fine by tomorrow.'

Azhar and Dr Sharif left the veranda and entered Judge Anwar's bedroom. Asgri sat on the bed, surrounded by women. As the men entered Asgri wiped her eyes and rearranged her stole to fully cover her head.

Azhar, seeing her tears, said, 'You shouldn't pay attention to Zafri, apa. He's just careless, uneducated. I'll talk to him later.'

Asgri rejected the comment. She said to one of the women by her side: 'It's not even seven days yet, but I understand that to others it seems like a long time already.' The woman nodded, shutting her eyes theatrically. 'So much seems to have happened since then.'

The judge's daughters – all in white, linseed oil on their hair – were sitting amongst the women. One of the women looked at Azhar and clicked her fingers at the four older girls. Of an age now to be guarded from the eyes of the adult male, they got up silently and left the room. Azhar was not aware of the command but he had registered the distaste that his presence caused on some of the faces in the room.

'You came about the medicines, doctor?' Asgri addressed Dr Sharif. The physician answered with a nod, guiltily. The bottles of vibrantly coloured pills, the eggshell-thin vials of injections and the packs of syringes and needles had all been collected in a large box. Dr Sharif took the box from the table and, to avoid having to wrestle with the beggars who were now filling the courtyard, he left by the inside door, emerging on to the back street – the door Judge Anwar would squat by to urinate at night.

It was hot, despite the absence of the sun and despite the fact that it had rained continuously for the past six or seven hours. Azhar pulled the collar of his shirt away from his neck and blew cold breath on to his chest. He sat down on the edge of the only empty chair in the room. With his head bowed and in an unvarying tone of voice, as though reading aloud from a book on his lap, he explained to Asgri the stage which the legal action against the judge's killers had reached and assured her that he, personally, was supervising the proceedings.

When he finished, Asgri shifted her eyes from her husband's photograph and nodded briskly. 'Yes,' she said. 'But, Azhar, there is something else. I want you to look through and sort out the papers in the safe. My brothers will need your help and advice when they come back for the tenth-day memorial service on Saturday. We've made some decisions. I'm selling everything and going back to Sind. There's nothing for me here.' She spoke quietly and softly.

The women let out sighs of protest.

'No.' Asgri smoothed away a wrinkle in the guipure counterpane. 'My mind's made up. Everything including the house.' Asgri was from a large feudal family in the south whose landholdings had been in the family for over three hundred years – since a century before the arrival of the British. An only sister to six brothers, Asgri was dearly loved. It was said that the brothers had been outraged to the point of threatening annulment on discovering, soon after the wedding ceremony, that Judge Anwar smoked cigarettes – something the judge had failed to declare when asking for their sister's hand in marriage.

Azhar stood up. 'I'll come by later, apa.'

'Be in time for dinner,' Asgri told him and he nodded. He was aware that some of the women were staring at him with quiet yet defiant hostility.

He turned to Nabila Ali and asked: 'Is Mujeeb Ali at home today, apa?'

Nabila's eyes hardened before she answered.

Azhar whispered a *salam-a-lekum* to all the women and left the room.

Zafri had spread a straw mat on the tiles of the veranda and was beginning to cut the meat on a block of tree trunk. He was dividing the quartered carcasses into smaller pieces by efficient strokes of the cleaver, as though attempting a children's puzzle where a minimum number of intersecting lines must be drawn inside a circle to achieve the maximum number of divisions. 'The poor animal lost its life and you still complain,' he said loudly, shaking his head in mock despair when one of the crowd of beggars asked for more than she had been given.

As Azhar walked past the tailor's shop – a roughly knocked together box of old boards whose corrugated-iron roof was shaking to the rattle of sewing machines – he heard his name being called out.

It was Saif Aziz. He emerged from the shop, clicking open his umbrella and raising an arm in greeting. Azhar waited under a tree as the journalist jumped over puddles towards him.

'Ah,' Azhar responded as Saif Aziz introduced himself and they shook hands. 'I know who you are.' They walked along the street, protected by the umbrella. 'You are the person who began printing the countdown to the General's election-within-ninety-days promise.'

Saif Aziz shrugged. In the newspaper that Saif Aziz had edited four years ago, the countdown to the General's promised election-day had appeared daily at the foot of the front page, in a large boxed inset. *The elections will be held within the next 28 days, 27 days, 26 days* . . . until, a fortnight before day zero, the newspaper was shut down.

'I intended to go into minus figures,' Saif Aziz smiled. '*The elections were held yesterday, two days ago, three days ago* . . .'

They were walking towards the courthouse. At the other side of the street a beggar woman with a pick-a-backed child, and a bulging sack slung over her shoulder, was directing another beggar to Judge Anwar's house.

'But I do safe work now,' said Saif Aziz. 'I have three children to feed and clothe. Though if the General's recent speeches are anything to go by, they'll soon shut down every newspaper in the country under the pretext that they're publishing letters of the alphabet that can be rearranged to form an anti-government message.'

Azhar said, 'Why are you telling *me* this? I myself try to be as honest as my position allows.'

But Saif Aziz continued on his former line. 'I'll tell you something which troubles me at night, deputy-sahib. This is the worst government we've ever had and yet this is the only government in my adult life under which I haven't been to prison.'

They walked on in silence until they came to the school building at the fork at the end of the street and stopped. The smell of decay, of putrefaction was overwhelming here. Water was seeping into the foundations of the school and rotting the underlay further. Water lizards crawled out from between the cracks at the base of the outside wall and scuttled about the street.

'So what can I do for you?' Azhar asked Saif Aziz.

'People aren't being very co-operative. No one is admitting to having actually received one of those letters. All they want to talk about is who they *think* has got one and what might be in it. Someone even said that one of the maulanas, Hafeez, has received one which he had written to his wife in his less older days, a letter full of love and longing.'

Azhar raised his shoulders. 'Why are you journalists always chasing after weird stories? Why can't you write about ordinary things?'

Saif Aziz made the umbrella rotate above their heads. 'To write about ordinary things is the duty of a novelist: it's the task of the journalist to write about extraordinary things.' He grinned.

'Who said that?' Azhar snapped his fingers a few times in an effort to remember. He poked Saif Aziz's chest. 'That Irishman . . . what was his name . . .?'

The other smiled. 'James Joyce.'

'Yes, James Joyce.'

Saif Aziz leaned towards Azhar's face. 'Should I write about the unusual manner in which the letters were delivered here?' His voice had quietened to a conspiratorial whisper.

Azhar came out from under the umbrella. 'If you must write about unusual things then go and write about that goat which I hear has been born with the Prophet's name on its hide.'

Saif Aziz reached out his hand and took Azhar by the upper arm. 'One more thing, deputy-sahib,' he said with a broad smile. 'I would be interested in knowing what attracts a deputy commissioner to a miserable place like this.'

Azhar freed himself gently. He began to cross to the street that would take him to the courthouse.

'You see, deputy-sahib,' Saif Aziz shouted after him. 'When I ask an ordinary question, no one makes a reply. They just walk away.'

Alice came to the kitchen door and shouted Zébun's name, calling down to the bedroom. There were two pans on the cooking range, and to avoid contaminating the dessert with the smell of spices she needed another pair of hands.

'You know how fussy Kasmi-sahib is when it comes to food,' Alice said as Zébun came and stood alongside her. Zébun stirred the bubbling milk. On the shelf by the range was a peeled orange whose rind had been added to the meat. In a glass of water Alice had dissolved a little food colouring; there were fresh coriander leaves resembling a duck's webbed feet, and rhomboids of glacé pumpkin – Sikh-yellow, bride-red.

Zébun looked into the pan of meat in front of Alice. 'Make sure to take out any big cardamoms from brother-ji's plate,' she advised the girl. 'He says they remind him of cockroaches.'

Alice smiled and sucked her teeth. Her lips were painted red. She glanced down at Zébun's feet and, beaming, said, 'You're wearing the new slippers.' And with a self-congratulatory look she added, 'I chose the design myself.'

Zébun continued to watch the tiny whirlpools that her stirring produced in the milk.

'I only wear high heels myself. I don't like flat slippers,' Alice was saying. 'I'm glad I'm not tall, or I wouldn't be able to wear high heels. I'm going to buy a new pair next Sunday. It's got rhinestones all along the edges. They say it's all the rage in the cities.'

She picked up the salt, tilted it above the meat and held it there. Zébun was about to comment on the imprudence of this when with a measured flick of the wrist Alice cut off the flow of the white crystals. She was half smiling and excitedly recounting the details of a recent afternoon when, she claimed, a young man had deliberately bumped into her walking down the street.

' "Can't you see?" I turned around and said sharply. And he answered back, "Of course I can see, that's why I bumped into you." ' She shook her head as though despairing. 'Men are terrible. Always bothering pretty girls.' She laughed.

Zébun was staring at Alice. Her eyes moved steadily from the gaudy clothes to the row of plastic beads around the neck and on to the untidily painted lips. 'Why do you wear that stuff on your lips, girl?' she said wearily. 'It's almost as if you needed to know where your mouth was. It's too hot for surkhi and powder anyway.'

Alice's laughter stopped abruptly. Zébun glanced up at her eyes and found herself looking at tears. She let her gaze fall instantly, pretending not to have seen. But the girl realised that she had been seen; she turned off the heat and began to weep openly.

Zébun stood motionless, shocked. Then she too turned off the heat under her pan. 'What's the matter, Alice?' Zébun remembered that something similar had happened a few years back when Alice had just begun to menstruate. The terrified girl had wept inconsolably, thinking she was going to die. Zébun had had to explain to her the changes taking place inside her twelve-year-old body. On that occasion Zébun had instantly guessed the cause of Alice's fear. And she had begun saving cloth for her – old towels, scraps and cuttings of dress material. Now she folded her arms and tried to think.

Alice turned her head from side to side – 'Nothing.' She shook her head again and tucked behind her ear a lock of hair that had escaped the pin. But then she placed both hands over her face and began to sob again, violently.

'Has brother-ji said anything?'

Alice dried her cheeks, blew her nose on her stole and swallowed hard. 'It's my father.'

The wrinkles on Zébun's forehead became pronounced. 'Is he unwell?'

Alice stared at the wall in front of her. 'No,' she managed to say before her eyes filled with tears once again. A droplet hung at the tip of her nose.

Zébun lost her temper. 'What then?'

Alice spoke with one hand still covering her face, as though she wished to hide it. 'I heard him talking to my mother. I was in the next room.'

A simple idea came to Zébun. She nodded and smiled. 'Are they looking for a suitable young man for you?' she asked and said, 'Well, Alice, all we women have one day to—'

'It's not that,' Alice interrupted softly. She inhaled rapidly through her mouth and tried to steady her breathing. 'I was in the next room and I heard my father say to my mother that she had given birth to an ugly daughter. He said every time he looks at me he wonders what kind of djinn or bhoot I am. And I heard him spit in the corner of the room.'

Zébun let herself watch the floor, silent as she tried to grasp what Alice was saying.

'And he did mention marriage. He said he wonders how he'll ever get rid of me. He said we're so poor we can't even tempt anybody with a large dowry.'

She leaned towards Zébun, perhaps asking to be held. But Zébun did not move.

A few minutes passed before Alice stopped her swaying and uncovered her face. Her eyes were red and her mouth was smudged. Wet from her tears was trapped in tiny films under the curving hairs of her face. She lit the fire under the meat. Zébun took a step back to allow her to light the second burner with the same matchstick. Their eyes did not meet.

Zébun said, 'Wipe your eyes, girl. Brother-ji is home, he might come in.'

'All we need to do is to appoint a new watchman, that's all.'

Mujeeb Ali opened the cupboard and, from the section neatly stacked with documents, he took out a file. 'It will take you a long time to understand how things are done in this place, Azhar.'

Azhar, seated behind the desk, took the fountain pen out of his pocket and unscrewed the cap. Mujeeb Ali brought the file over to the desk and placed it unopened before him. 'How was Gul-kalam chosen?' Azhar asked.

Mujeeb Ali took the empty chair across the desk. 'No one remembers. He used to supply firewood to people's houses and sometimes milk the cows. Over the years he became the night-watchman and brought his family down from the mountains. His brother began painting houses. Just one of those things.'

Azhar opened the file and, without reading, scrawled his signature at the bottom of the page. He lifted the corner of the first sheet and signed the next page. 'It shouldn't be your exclusive decision as to who guards the town at night,' he said without raising his eyes from the papers. 'Who are these people anyway? I'm not sure I feel comfortable with the idea of four armed men roaming the streets at night.' His voice was courteous, but strained.

Mujeeb Ali listened patiently, unblinking. 'It's not just my men. There were two policemen with them last night, as there will be tonight.'

Since it was Tuesday Azhar had spent the afternoon at the court-house hearing criminal cases brought by the magistrate. It was the only time of the week when he was sure to be in town. A deputy commissioner had to preside over the weekly sessions court in every town under his command: so even if Azhar had lived else-where he would have had to journey to this town once a week. Otherwise Azhar kept erratic hours, arrived and left whenever he wished. So every Tuesday there was a barrage of people congesting the arches outside the courthouse, as they waited to see him: there were those who needed passports and identity cards for departures to the Arab countries; others offering bribes to secure a favourable outcome of cases; fathers of unemployed sons, mothers of nubile daughters; sharecroppers needing loans to buy oxen. For the rest of the week these people would leave messages and gifts outside his house – baskets of fruit and vegetables, sides of meat, embroidery and lace, cakes of white perfumed soap, cages of songbirds. Once there was a fighting cock with a plucked neck and a tiny canvas muzzle over its beak, and once, even more surprising, there was a large bouquet of flowers. In the beginning Azhar used to send these things to the mosques but then it began to seem easier just to drag them over the threshold. People also approached him through Mujeeb Ali.

Tired and hungry he closed the file and looked Mujeeb Ali straight in the eye. 'And I would like your men out of the post office.' The noises of the heaving river outside the house and the heat were making it difficult for him to breathe.

A curt smile came to Mujeeb Ali's lips.

Azhar spoke again: 'If anything needed to be done I would have authorised it. Any order would have gone from me to the superintendent of police and from him to the police inspector. *He* should have carried it out.'

Mujeeb Ali picked up the file. 'So,' he said, 'you don't approve of what I did?'

'No.' Azhar returned the pen to his pocket. 'You are just a citizen. It was outside your jurisdiction.' Then immediately, as though it only needed mentioning – was not to be lingered on, not to be stressed by allowing a silence to mount up – he lowered his voice and said, 'You must try to understand my position. The town is without a post office now. I have divisional superiors to report back to. And since the suspension of the Constitution I am also answerable to the provincial martial-law administrator.'

Mujeeb Ali laughed indulgently. 'Is that what bothers you?' Expression had returned to his face. 'Your divisional superior, as you so respectfully address him, and my brother Nadir used to play marbles outside this very house. Nothing has really changed since then except that now they play polo on the General's private grounds.'

The words came out in a shout. 'That is not the point.'

'Calm yourself, Azhar. You were not here and the matter had to be dealt with urgently.'

'Urgently? There is nothing here that needs to be taken the least bit seriously.' Azhar had stood up, straining forwards, his palms splayed on the desktop.

Raindrops hurled themselves against the glass of the window. From the quality of the light Azhar sensed that it was past five o'clock. He walked around the desk. 'I have to go now,' he said lightly.

Mujeeb Ali's eyes followed him unseeingly to the door. 'I'll have the post office keys sent to the barracks.'

Azhar turned at the door and showed him his empty palms. 'You have to understand my position.'

The weather showed no signs of lifting. Smoky, silver-edged clouds piled up above the house. Plants thrashed in the gale and the rainwater corkscrewed down from the eaves and clapped on the edge of the parquet veranda. Arshad Ali was on the veranda with his niece when Mujeeb Ali emerged from the door behind them. Uncle and niece appeared to be discussing the parrot hanging above their heads. Arshad Ali pointed at the bird through the parallel bars at the base of the cage. 'Does it talk?'

The girl shook her head vigorously. She had her little arms locked tightly around her uncle Arshad's neck. 'The man who sold it to us said it would talk since it had a band of black feathers around its neck. But that was painted on,' the child explained singingly.

Arshad Ali adopted the same sing-song voice: 'Well, you had better keep it away from my falcons because they eat parrots. One of them is from the same clutch of eggs as three birds belonging to the king of Saudi Arabia. It has fourteen feathers in its tail.'

126

Mujeeb Ali approached. 'How long are you staying this time?'

Arshad Ali did not look up. 'I don't know,' he mumbled. He had arrived just before dawn, after an absence of eleven months, bringing with him several cages of hawks, falcons and eagles. He had spent the months in the north-west, living amongst tribesmen.

The girl lifted her head and inclined it sideways, her eyes and mouth rounded in anticipation. 'I hear someone,' she whispered. The door opened and Nabila came in.

'Go inside, son,' Nabila told her daughter who had rushed to greet her. 'Find your sisters.'

Mujeeb Ali, standing till now, sat down in the cane chair.

Nabila curled her lips. 'That deputy commissioner was here again, wasn't he?' She addressed her husband. 'He asked me whether you were home and I couldn't lie.'

Mujeeb Ali gave a nod. 'Yes, he was here.' There were lines across his forehead, intersected at the bridge of the nose by a deep vertical indentation. Nabila watched him anxiously. 'Ji, Asgri is selling everything and going back to Sind. Everything – the shares in the mines, the land, the houses.'

Again an uncertain nod.

A group of servant girls, carrying mosquito nettings and bamboo poles, was crossing the length of the opposite veranda. The froth-like nettings were light and diaphanous and from this side the girls looked as though they were hidden by smears and smudges of white paint.

'Keep your ducks and hens locked up from now on,' Arshad Ali shouted across the courtyard. His gaze stayed with the girls until they disappeared into one of the bedrooms. Then he turned to his brother: 'I bumped into Tahir, Saji, Alli and Kamal when I got in last night. I'll join them on the patrol tonight.'

Mujeeb Ali touched his armpit and asked, 'Have you got your . . .?'

Arshad Ali nodded and touched the hard metal of the gun beneath the fabric of his own shirt.

Nabila said, 'I want you to be careful with that thing. You used to go patrolling during the elections and I remember what used to happen then.'

❧

On Sunday, after seeing Maulana Hafeez washing the floor – his trousers rolled up to mid-shin, his elastic-strapped wristwatch pushed up to the elbow – Mujeeb Ali had sent two servants to the mosque. Maulana Hafeez had initially objected to the appointment as wasteful extravagance but had finally agreed to take on one of the boys.

'It's the same every year,' the cleric murmured to himself as he instructed the boy to keep the courtyard door shut against the invading water lizards, to prevent the soiling of the prayer-mats.

Magrib was said in the hall, the space being big enough for the handful of men. After the prayers, instead of collecting their shoes and leaving, the men gathered around Maulana Hafeez.

Eagerly, Maulana Hafeez straightened his spine against the wooden steps of the mimber, the pulpit.

'Maulana-ji, we have an important matter to discuss with you.'

Maulana Hafeez lowered his head while his hand patted the velvet of the prayer-mat, feeling for the rosary, in ever-widening arcs.

'It's the matter of the deputy commissioner and that girl.'

Maulana Hafeez nodded, his eyes shut.

'It's setting a bad example for the whole town, Maulana-ji.' Maulana Hafeez recognised the voice. 'We all have daughters and sisters. If we allow the DC and that girl to continue then we could be said to be condoning this sort of behaviour.'

'And others might be encouraged, Maulana-ji. It's almost as if we are telling them that we tolerate such sinners,' someone near the back said.

Maulana Hafeez raised a quelling hand. 'I myself have been giving a great deal of thought to this matter and there are a number of ways which I think will lead to a satisfactory solution. However . . .'

Someone raised himself to his knees: 'I own that house, Maulana-ji. I didn't know what kind of a man he was when I let it to him. Since I am the owner of the property he's implicating me in his sin.'

'You won't have to worry about that for long. I have a feeling he's going to buy Judge Anwar's house from the widow and live there with that girl.'

'They say he has a wife and two children in Lahore. That's why he's away all the time.'

Maulana Hafeez raised his hand again. 'Nothing has been proved yet. But as I was saying—'

'Everything has been proved, Maulana-ji. She has moved in with him. She was seen by half the street buying vegetables on the doorstep.'

Another disembodied voice rose: 'If it was merely gossip we wouldn't have troubled you, Maulana-ji. But now we have proof.'

'The Qur'an categorically states that a Muslim is not to befriend a Christian.' A timid voice issued from the huddle of men. 'So it's twice as sinful.'

'That's true.' Maulana Hafeez brushed his beard with his fingers. 'But have you forgotten what the Almighty said to Hazrat Ibraheem when he turned away a non-Muslim from his table? The Almighty said, Ibraheem, I have provided for that man for so many years despite the fact that he is not a believer, are you so righteous that you couldn't even feed him for just one day?'

'But, Maulana-ji, that's different.'

'Indeed it is. But remember that every sura of the Qur'an begins with the words, Allah the Compassionate, the Merciful.' And at a meditative pace Maulana Hafeez recited, from memory, a passage concerning adultery from the holy book. *Unless he repent and do good works, for then God will change his sins to good actions – God is forgiving and merciful – he that repents and does good works shall truly return to God.*

The men listened in silence as the cleric translated.

As he finished, Maulana Hafeez said, 'Leave this with me. You'll see that the matter will be resolved within the next few days, by gentle persuasion.'

The men made brief humming noises. Maulana Hafeez continued more solemnly still, 'But surely before turning to others we must examine ourselves.' He waved a hand over the heads of the men. 'There was a time when we needed the hall and the veranda *and* the courtyard to contain all the men who came to the mosque. Now there aren't even enough of you to fill the hall.'

'But, forgive me, Maulana-ji, that was a time when there was only one mosque in the town.'

'That is beside the point. We seem to have found many distractions. So many songs coming out of the radios, so many televisions. You can't tell me that *that's* setting a good example.'

Someone said tentatively: 'Maulana-ji, people are afraid to leave their homes because last night Mujeeb Ali's men were patrolling the streets once again. From now on, no one is going to leave their home after sunset.'

The maulana refused the explanation. 'That's fanciful,' he smiled into his lap.

'They were outside my house from two till four-thirty, laughing and playing cards. They urinated standing up against the pharmacy door.'

'It will be like the elections when they beat us up saying we were on our way to someone's house for a secret meeting.'

Maulana Hafeez asked for silence. 'It will be nothing like those months. The whole country is now blessed by the grace of God. The General is a God-fearing man and, as a result, for the first time in over a decade there is peace and prosperity.'

The statement was met with silence.

All day, Maulana Hafeez had been aware of a papiha's singing; it was now somewhere just outside the mosque. 'As for this town,' he continued, 'it is going to be safer than ever in a few months' time. It will be fortified, like a castle, once the gates have gone up.'

'Gates, Maulana-ji?'

Maulana Hafeez nodded earnestly. He had intended to include the news in his Friday sermon. Mujeeb Ali, he explained, had decided that every street in town was to have, at either end, huge cast-iron gates. The gates would be locked at night by the nightwatchman – still to be chosen – who would be responsible for the keys. Every household was expected to contribute something, although the bulk of the cost would be borne by the Alis.

'The gates will be unlocked by the nightwatchman at the end of his rounds at dawn,' Maulana Hafeez smiled contentedly. 'It will be like living in the walled city of some Mogul emperor, at a time when Islam ruled the entire subcontinent – before the arrival of the degenerate British.' And, with a grappling gesture, he tugged the folds of his robe to himself. A furious smile played in his eyes.

*Mother promises she'll buy me a whole rupee's worth of falsé if the postman calls today. She is expecting a letter. I sit on the doorstep. The postmark is five wavy, river-like lines across the top of the envelope, overlapping the stamp. Father has gone away to find work in Saudi Arabia. Mother had to sell her bangles and her necklace and the five-fingered punjangala. If the postman likes a stamp he tears it off, and the letter arrives in an envelope which has one corner missing.*

*The flowers of ishq-é-péchan grow in clusters. Each flower has five petals at the end of a long hollow stalk. The thin stalk can be bent into a circle and inserted into the hole at the centre of the five petals. A wedding ring. Rings can be looped into each other to make a chain – a necklace for the bride or a garland for the bridegroom.*

*Nothing used to grow in the courtyard. Then Sujata told Mother to pour sheep's blood on to the soil. The blood came in an aluminium bucket. In the bucket, and on the soil, the blood looked dark, almost black; but during its journey from the tilted bucket to the barren soil it was bright red – ruby-coloured. A bucketful was added every month. And now we have jasmine and seven-winged gul-é-lala in the courtyard. Birds come*

131

to eat the nectar. A young bird pecks at a dry seed concealed in the webbing of a mat.

Sujata and Mother grew up together. After Father left, Mother told her her dreams. She seemed to fall through a hole, and continued to fall for such a long time that, above her head, the rim of the hole disappeared . . . Nothing but darkness, and yet she still kept falling.

She stops by on her way back from the bazaar and tells Mother who she saw at the shops. She buys satin ribbons and dragonfly hair-clips for my hair. She makes two plaits – four-stranded! – and arranges one before the shoulder and the other behind. She paints my lips red and inserts a sprig of lilac into my hair, just above the nape of the neck. And then she plants a kiss on my forehead. A tiny silver snake holds her index finger in a fivefold embrace. Her fingernails look like rose petals.

Sujata's bangles chime inside the room. Mother is laughing.

Mimosa encircles the window frame, the leaflets sparkling in the sunlight. The thin branches are held up by strings tied to drawing-pins pushed into the wall. Some strings have lost their colour – bleached away by the sun; others were recently put up, attached to the younger branches. Purple flowers peer into the room. Mimosa leaves react if you touch them; the leaves snap shut like a Japanese fan. I look through the glass into the room. The mimosa leaves contract at the touch of my skin, and light enters the room – a small blue clearing in the darkened room. Sujata's mükaished stole is on the floor. Her arms are wrapped around Mother's body; their lips touch each other. Behind them, on the shelf, the yellow rose swivels through an arc in its vase, almost as though it's stretching and yawning. Father's picture looks down into the room, one shoulder higher than the other.

The postman knocks on the door. Birds fly above the courtyard in curved paths like sagging marquee roofs. Singing, they cut the air into strips with their scissor beaks. I take the letter into the room. When you step out of the sun into the shade your forearms notice the cold before the rest of you. Sujata's face is covered in flaky pink powder as though she had opened a large box and a thousand butterflies had rushed out, leaving rainbow dust on her skin. Mother reads the letter. Father says he'll be home for Eid this year. He will bring a television. He tells Mother she is not to hit me, ever, 'not even with a flower on a stem'.

*The night before he left, Mother says, he stayed awake and stroked my face and hair. Sujata is eating a hill-station apple, her fingers curved around the fruit like the little prongs that hold a ruby in a ring. Her brother-in-law also went away to work and has sent them a television and a camera. In the evening me, Lubna, Uzma, Aamar, Mitho, Sabahat and Farzana go to Sujata's house to watch cartoons.*

*Wednesday*

—

Slow and awkward, Yusuf Rao negotiated the puddles outside the barber shop. The rain had long ceased and a hot Wednesday was emerging – a Wednesday not much different from the previous one. Swollen drains drowned the edges of the street. The acrid grey water was still, except directly above the openings of the drains where the escaping jets caused great wrinkles. Inside the shop the barber sat sweltering in the heat – the electricity had been cut off sometime during the night and the fan was not working. He was practising the trick with the charged comb that had appeared in the children's supplement last week.

'Making your own electricity, Nabi?' Yusuf Rao said as he climbed on to the platform.

The barber let drop the comb covered in tiny squares of paper and stood up. 'Ah, a customer,' he said good-humouredly. 'Even if he *is* a lawyer.'

Yusuf Rao stepped squarely into the shop and commented on the heat before settling in the chair. The barber folded down the collar of Yusuf Rao's shirt, tucking it into the shirt. Then he wrapped him in a white sheet. The sheet was cut like a woman's dress pattern, or like a side of meat.

'It *is* hot,' he said over the click of the scissors. 'It's a time for sleeping out on the veranda. But we've been sleeping behind locked doors since last week.'

Yusuf Rao murmured a mild curse. 'What a mess. And all because of some silly letters.'

The barber rebuked him gently for the bad language. 'Isfahan Butt has sent his wife back to her parents, without the children. Apparently, it has something to do with those letters.'

Yusuf Rao forced his head up. '*Apparently?*' he smiled. 'According to whom?'

The barber pushed his head back down.

'That's how rumours start, Nabi.' Yusuf Rao laughed into the folds of the wrap; he was sweating.

The barber went to the shelf to exchange the scissors. The new pair chirruped like a metal sparrow. Five minutes later the barber required Yusuf Rao to lift his head. 'Are you asleep?'

Yusuf Rao stirred. 'At our age you're only getting out of bed to find another comfortable place to fall asleep in.'

The barber came round to the front and began to shape the greying hair on the forehead. Using the comb he smoothed the hairs into shallow curves before clipping the uneven tips.

At that moment, Maulana Hafeez tapped softly on the pane. The barber had looked up at the sound of footsteps advancing along the platform. Now his eyes shot towards the bench, where the radio was concealed.

After the greetings – the barber was reverent, Yusuf Rao restrained – the cleric went to sit on the bench.

'Now,' Maulana Hafeez said through a drawn-out sigh, 'have you heard the news about the gates?'

The barber shook his head; Yusuf Rao loosened the wrap around his neck.

When Maulana Hafeez finished explaining the plan, Yusuf Rao threw his head back against the head-rest and laughed, clipped hair tumbling off his draped shoulders. The barber, sitting by the maulana's side, looked disconsolately first at Yusuf Rao and then at Maulana Hafeez.

'Forgive me, Maulana-ji,' Yusuf Rao contained his laughter, 'but that is the most absurd proposal I've ever heard.' He tried not to look at Maulana Hafeez.

Maulana Hafeez hesitated before speaking. 'But the town would be a safer place then.'

Yusuf Rao resisted the temptation to demur. The barber was nodding eagerly.

Maulana Hafeez went on: 'It's best to be prepared. This time eight days ago no one knew that Judge Anwar would be killed.'

Yusuf Rao sought Maulana Hafeez in the mirror. For a moment their eyes met, then both looked away. 'In a way, Maulana-ji, I did,' the lawyer said sourly. 'He got what he deserved, had punishment meted out to him for all his crimes. Isn't that what the Qur'an says about criminals, Maulana-ji?'

In a self-conscious effort to lighten the situation the barber said, 'Maulana-ji, what would happen to the roaming herds of cows and water buffaloes when the gates go up?'

Maulana Hafeez did not reply.

'There is a term in the English language that sums up this scheme beautifully, Maulana-ji,' Yusuf Rao said. 'Hare-brained. It means rash and foolish.' And he roared with laughter once more.

Maulana Hafeez said, 'This concerns everyone in the town. It's a matter of your own safety too, Yusuf.'

'I've already had one brush with death, Maulana-ji. It doesn't bother me.'

Maulana Hafeez said in a low voice, 'You're being wilful simply because you still think that it was Mujeeb Ali who had you shot. But you must remember how strongly the Qur'an speaks out against defamation.'

Yusuf Rao examined the cleric – the white cap, the small bony face bearing the ravages of over seventy summers, the venerable white beard, the spotless white shirt smoothed meticulously with the palm of the hand before sitting down and beneath whose fabric the outline of a vest could be made out; an impassioned old man, the single-mindedness of whose passion had never ceased to surprise him. He spoke softly, 'The world isn't as simple as you are determined to see it, Maulana-ji. Not any more. You must recognise that some people have a heavy investment in causing hate.'

The reply was firm. 'I cannot believe that. No matter how complicated the world becomes there is still only one absolute truth.'

Yusuf Rao too was shaking his head. He sighed and said, 'Anyway, Maulana-ji, you can tell Mujeeb Ali that I'm not contributing even a teddy-paisa towards this scheme.'

He was not heard. There were loud voices outside the shop. The barber stood up slowly, reluctantly, and went to the door. The newspaper photographer was on the other side of the street, surrounded by a group of men and children. He appeared to be asking for instructions and it was clear that he was receiving contradictory or unsatisfactory answers. Maulana Hafeez approached the door. Only then did the barber see that one side of the photographer's face and most of the upper part of his shirt were covered in blood.

Maulana Hafeez's loud exclamation caused Yusuf Rao to come to the door as quickly as he was able. The photographer saw them come out of the shop and hurried across the street.

'What happened?' Yusuf Rao took off the cloth which was still wrapped around his body. With a nod of approval from the barber he offered it to the photographer. 'Did you have a fall?'

The cut was high on the forehead, near the hairline. Drops of blood formed at the point of the injured man's chin, two had fallen on to the camera slung around his neck. 'Does this town have a doctor?' he said testily.

Maulana Hafeez touched his elbow. 'What happened?'

'I went to photograph that goat. A woman hit me with an iron rod saying I was taking away the animal's soul.'

Maulana Hafeez said quietly, 'Islam forbids us to make images of God's creatures. On the Last Day, God will challenge all artists to breathe life into what they created. Forced to admit failure, they will be consigned to the Fire.'

The injured man gasped in anger. 'Maulana-sahib, you have been to Mecca, haven't you? Well, then, didn't you have a photograph taken for your passport?'

'But that was not for vanity,' said Maulana Hafeez, unperturbed. 'And the first thing I did on getting back from the pilgrimage was to burn the passport.' And with that he took the photographer's elbow. 'I'll take you to Dr Sharif.' He guided the man along the street. The photographer, holding the cloth to his forehead, let himself be led.

'I had to see Azhar about something very important but that will have to wait now,' said Maulana Hafeez.

Someone from the crowd shouted after him: 'I have just seen his car drive away, Maulana-ji. So don't trouble yourself today.'

Another voice rose, causing Maulana Hafeez to look back with a heavy heart. 'You could always leave a message, Maulana-ji. Someone's bound to be home.'

Yusuf Rao watched the cleric's receding back. 'I was wrong when I said Maulana Hafeez doesn't understand the complexity of the world. I think he does. He just embraces the lesser of two evils when it suits him, and at other times absolutely refuses to compromise. It's the other maulana, Maulana Dawood, the fanatic, who doesn't realise that times have changed.'

'But Maulana Dawood has been to Mecca as well,' the barber said. 'Five times.'

'I wonder if he burns his passport every time he gets back.'

'Maybe he knows he will be needing it again and keeps it.'

Back inside, the barber finished trimming Yusuf Rao's hair. Then he smoothed shaving foam on to the lower half of Yusuf Rao's face – Yusuf Rao gripped his lips between his teeth – and, after testing the razor on his callused palm, got ready to shave him. Yusuf Rao released his lips: they were neatly defined by the white foam.

'I forgot to mention,' the barber said. 'On Saturday Kasmi-sahib and Maulana Hafeez nearly bumped into each other. Right here. Kasmi-sahib saw Maulana-ji but I don't think that Maulana-ji saw *him*.' He pushed his glasses up his nose with the back of his wrist, the razor pointing in the air. He moved Yusuf Rao's chin upwards and began to shave the stretched skin under the jaw.

Yusuf Rao was unable to speak so the barber continued: 'They burned his whole family. I often wonder what poor Kasmi-sahib felt having just heard the news about his village and then listening to the two maulana-jis rejoicing on their loudspeakers that the country was being purged.'

With a forefinger Yusuf Rao pushed the razor away from his face, slowly and evenly as though on a smooth rail. 'Maulana

141

Hafeez had nothing to do with that. He was in Mecca during those months. Remember? It was Maulana Dawood and the temporary maulana of this mosque who gave those sermons.'

'So do you think Maulana Hafeez would have acted differently?'

A faint, almost imperceptible, breeze was at work. All around them branches were letting go of leaves. Suraya bent down to pick one up, then looked around and through the drizzle of yellow leaves located the small tree growing against the courtyard wall to which the leaf had belonged until only moments ago.

'Did that apricot ever give any fruit?' she asked Kalsum. Since there was no electricity they were sitting in the cool of the veranda. Birds sang in their cages – some suspended from the ceiling, others in a line at the edge of the brick floor.

'You remember,' Kalsum said, surprised. 'When your brother-ji bought it he thought it was an apricot tree but as it turned out he'd made a mistake. It is a peach tree. The first year it produced only flowers, no fruit. So we changed its position and the following year it did produce fruit, peaches!'

The garden was fading fast for the coming winter. The grape-vine was nothing more now than a tangled mesh of thin branches which looked like rust-covered wire. Years before – from the time she had been widowed until the year of her son's death – Kalsum would, in early summer, have tiny sacks of cloth tied over the choicest bunches of grapes, to prevent birds from pecking at the fruit. Enough fruit was left, though, for the humming-birds that were so fond of visiting the garden. She had made the sacks by cutting up an old dress.

'That' – she pointed at the lubinium – 'is a cutting we got from Gul-kalam.' Gul-kalam had brought some saplings from the mountains to plant outside his house and being native to higher altitudes the plant was beginning to turn green. During December and January the whole plant would be smothered in blazing yellow petals.

'Flowers in winter,' Suraya said quietly. 'When I left for England I thought I'd never see flowers again. I hadn't seen many flowers in winter here and I knew that England was a *very* cold country.' And she looked at her sister and said: 'There *are* flowers in those countries but you still dream of the place you come from.'

'It's easy to dream when your stomach is full,' Kalsum said. 'Don't forget you left this country because you didn't have anything to eat here. It didn't seem very pretty then, did it?'

Suraya looked away.

'I remember just after you were married,' Kalsum said, 'Burkat said he'd leave for England soon. Everybody was going in those days. He said he would make lots of money. "It's a rich country, England is, sister-in-law," he said.'

Suraya smiled painfully. 'He ended up in Canada, in a restaurant, washing dishes like a woman.'

'When he left he said the first thing he was going to do on reaching England was to employ a gora to clean his shoes. It was to be his revenge for the hundred and fifty years of their raj.'

Suraya twirled the yellow leaf in her hand, then she dropped it. She rubbed her fingertips together to dislodge any dirt. Her nails were bitten down to the quick. 'We didn't know anything,' she said. 'Neither of us.'

Kalsum touched her sister's arm. 'Go back to him.'

'I don't know what I should do,' Suraya said under her breath. And she repeated the words louder, as though she herself needed to hear them spoken.

By late afternoon Alice had managed to kill every water lizard in and around the house. The day had been hot and dry and she found most of them in the damp corners of the bathroom or in the moist soil of the flowerbeds. Mr Kasmi had to spend the whole afternoon listening to loud thuds as the broom descended on the witless creatures. Afterwards Alice sprinkled salt on the doorstep and, against Mr Kasmi's advice, blocked the drain-pipes with rags. At five o'clock, when the heat ebbed, she went out to throw the dead creatures into the river.

When the doorbell rang Mr Kasmi, who was searching for a favourite poem in an anthology, clicked his tongue in displeasure and put the book on the table. He went to the open window and looked down on to the street. Maulana Hafeez was standing on the doorstep.

Mr Kasmi waited for a few moments before stepping back. Then, after another brief pause, he crossed the room and went on to the landing. He saw that Zébun was on the courtyard below, excitedly welcoming the cleric into the house.

'Allah, Maulana-ji,' Zébun was saying, 'so you decided at last to bless this house with your presence.' Maulana Hafeez was smiling absently; he pointed to the doorstep and asked, 'Is this salt?' Zébun arranged her stole over her head. 'The water lizards, Maulana-ji. It's that girl's idea.' She steered Maulana Hafeez towards her bedroom.

Mr Kasmi returned to his room and picked up the book.

Maulana Hafeez had never visited the house before, not once. When word of Zébun's arrival spread through the town all those years ago, Maulana Hafeez had planned a visit. But before he could find time Zébun herself came to see him. She said she was carrying the child of a man who had promised to marry her but who, in the face of resistance from his wife and family, was now irresolute. Now he would only marry her if the child that she carried turned out to be a girl: the family, she said, could not trust her – a courtesan – with a female child. In the case of a boy she would receive a monthly allowance but there was to be no attempt at direct contact with the father. Zébun was visiting the cleric to ask what observances – special rosaries, specific verses of the Qur'an – could ensure a girl. It was an unusual wish. Women always came asking for a male child, and were told to recite daily the section of the Qur'an concerning Hazrat Ibraheem and his wish in old age for a son – a wish that was granted in Ishak. When the townspeople heard about the unusual wish, their fears

144

were confirmed: only a prostitute would wish for a girl. Evil charms were thrown into Zébun's courtyard. There were showers of mysterious seeds and pulses, small packets of powder, bottles of liquid that changed colour at the touch, scraps of paper with geometric designs and sequences of inverted numbers; and once a goat's ear was nailed to the window during the night. For all that the baby, a boy, lived for only a few hours.

Over the years Zébun had continued to visit Maulana Hafeez at his house. Maulana Hafeez was aware of the persecution she had suffered during her earlier years in the town. And he had been forced eventually – when he heard the rumour that Zébun's bathroom had a looking-glass floor – to include the matter in a Friday sermon. Without direct reference to Zébun he had talked at length about the spirit of tolerance and forbearance. He was understood.

When he heard Maulana Hafeez leave, Mr Kasmi came downstairs. Zébun was sitting inside the mosquito netting.

'What did Maulana Hafeez want, sister-ji?'

'They're thinking about putting up gates at either end of the street,' Zébun replied. And she explained the matter as best she could. 'That's how I understood it,' she concluded. 'You'd better ask the men about it, brother-ji.'

'Such a strange scheme.'

'Many people seem to have agreed. Dr Sharif, Nasin Hasanie, Majid and Wajid Shafik. And I too think that if it can prevent something like last week then it's worth the trouble and expense. But as I said, you better ask around; you're the man of the house, brother-ji.'

Mr Kasmi nodded.

Zébun said, 'Brother-ji, I hope Maulana Hafeez's being here didn't distress you. All these years I have gone to see Maulana-ji at his house, just to prevent him from coming here and maybe reminding you of – no, no, let me finish, brother-ji – but today I couldn't hide my pleasure at seeing Maulana-ji in the house, even though I knew you were standing watching by the banéra. I now realise that it was a little inappropriate.'

Mr Kasmi came into the room. 'Whoever else was responsible for those months, sister-ji, we can be sure it wasn't Maulana Hafeez. He was out of the country at the time.' Mr Kasmi remembered, as clearly as yesterday, the day he had seen an anti-Ahmadiya slogan for the first time. Through the window of his bedroom he had looked down on to the street and seen a boy squatting by the wall opposite. He had paints and brushes by his side and he was waiting for the white rectangle he had painted on the wall to dry. When next Mr Kasmi looked out through the papery flowers of the bougainvillaea – it was spring – the white background had words written on it, and the boy was long gone. Soon there would be stencils, and handbills, and leaflets dropped on to waving children from a blue aeroplane.

They were quiet for a few moments. Then Zébun reached her hand under the pillow. 'Brother-ji, I have something I would like you to see.'

Only when the envelope was out of the gloom cast by the mosquito netting did Mr Kasmi see that it was dark green in colour.

'Sister-ji! Who was it from?'

Zébun folded her arms across her stomach. 'From his wife. It was an invitation to their daughter's wedding.'

The sound of Alice's wooden heels resounded on the tiles. 'I decided to feed them to Bano's geese instead,' she shouted into the bedroom, explaining away her prolonged absence.

Zébun said quietly: 'You mean you felt like gossiping.' And loudly: 'Don't forget we're answerable to your parents for your safety, girl.'

It was a short letter, written in an elegant hand, and arranged into neat paragraphs. Mr Kasmi folded the paper. The smell of old paper – familiar to him from his volumes of Dickens, Wamaq Saleem and Virginia Woolf – wafted up.

'She called you sister,' he said and stood up to hand the letter back. 'What do you plan to do?'

'I don't know. It was written a long time ago.'

'Nineteen years ago.'

'He'd been dead five years when she wrote it. Why did she want to invite me to their daughter's wedding?'

Mr Kasmi was more direct this time: 'Do you plan to write, sister-ji?'

Zébun was tracing the edges of the envelope with a fingertip. 'We don't even know whether she's still alive, brother-ji.'

'The marshal eagle's escaped!' shouted one of the night-patrollers. They had gone into the shed by the stables to see the birds tethered on their perches. There were two golden falcons, four eagle hawks and four peregrines. Some – those which wore leather hoods over their heads – looked as though they were sculpted in wood.

The three-year-old marshal eagle was an obedient bird with a peaceable character and was seldom tied up. It had been bred in an aviary and had learned not to fly into the wire mesh. It was graceful with a five-foot wing span and never ate anything unless it was offered on the point of a dagger. During hunts it flew in a perfect circle for a long time – like the hand of a distinguished lady uncertain above a plate of sweetmeats, Arshad Ali had often said – before descending upon the selected morsel. In the mountains it could be trusted to come back from flights of considerable distance, and on several occasions had been left out overnight. But skies around the town were unfamiliar and Arshad Ali had tied it to the perch with a chain fixed with a metal half-moon link that was hammered shut.

The bird had broken the chain and flown out through one of the ventilation holes.

They did not have to search for long. Lining the wider streets of the town and the inner banks of both rivers were large talli trees, both sprawling and tall. It was in one of these, growing on the bank of the eastern river, that they located the eagle, desperately flapping its wings near the topmost branches. The chain which had become entangled in the branches had broken at the half-moon link and a considerable length was still attached to the bird's prehensile claw.

'She'll break a wing!' Arshad Ali climbed up as the bird struggled to free itself.

Evening was easing into night. The air was filled with the cries of alarmed birds who had returned from the day to find a predator near their nests. From high above their heads the four men heard the sound of wings striking the branches become suddenly louder, increase to a frenzy, then stop altogether: Arshad Ali had grabbed the chain, pulled the bird under his arm and stilled the beating wings. He held the claws – each the size of a human infant's hand and each prong ending in a razor-sharp hook – in one hand and began the long climb down. He had cleared the canopy of leaves and was almost at the base of the trunk when his left foot slipped from under him. He released the claws to steady himself against the trunk. The marshal eagle, equally instinctively, reached for the nearest object and embedded a claw deep into Arshad Ali's face.

He could not cry out. The bird fastened on his mouth with one talon hooked under the jaw and another through the upper lip; the remaining two were buried in the left side of the face. The skin on the cheekbone had been pulled down to reveal the flesh lining the eyeball. Arshad still held the bird firmly under the arm, its curved beak open to expose a tongue the colour, shape and size of a peeled almond.

'Get a knife. We'll have to kill her!'

Arshad Ali was making a dull grunting sound at the back of his throat, behind the clamped-shut mouth. The claw was turning red with blood. One of the men produced a large curved knife enveloped in a canvas sheath. Arshad Ali reached his hand to his jaw and with a sharp, desperate movement prised the back talon from under his chin. A jet of blood, dark blue in the failing light, soaked the front of the shirt.

'Don't kill her!' he shouted as soon as the jaw was free.

Working by the light of a torch they loosened the bird's ferocious grip. Two men took the eagle home while the other two, walking either side of Arshad Ali, accompanied him to Dr Sharif's house.

The physician was closing the door of the surgery. He took a step back into the room. 'And whose picture were *you* trying to take?' He turned around and hurried to the large screen on rubber wheels which he pushed aside to reveal a couch.

Arshad Ali forced a smile at the physician's comment. With a wave of his free hand – the other clasping the front of his shirt to the wounds – he sent the two men away. The surgery was divided into two sections by a large curtain; behind the curtain female patients would sit. On the wall above the couch was an old calendar depicting a Nigerian rural scene – a souvenir of the four years Dr Sharif had spent in Africa.

'What happened?' Dr Sharif asked as he approached the couch, collecting as he came a kidney-shaped receptacle holding a pair of scissors, gauze and a roll of surgical tape.

'One of my birds,' Arshad Ali managed to say before a spike of pain forced him to wince.

Dr Sharif examined the wounds. Three of the four gashes, each a three-quarter-inch tear, could be clearly seen; the fourth was hidden in the bristly moustache. 'You're lucky it wasn't an eye,' the physician said and pressed cottonwool to the cheek to absorb blood and the glistening beads of sweat. 'There's no need for stitches but you'll have to have a course of tetanus injections.' Dr Sharif dipped the cottonwool in the beaker of water. The water turned orange.

'There is something I have always wanted to know, doctor-sahib,' Arshad Ali said through stiff lips. 'When we were children we used to say that if a dog bit you, you had to have fourteen injections in your stomach. Is that true?'

Dr Sharif concentrated on his work. He had begun to feel along the edges of the wounds – clearly defined now that the excess blood had been swabbed up. Then he drenched a large piece of cottonwool in antiseptic solution and began to dress the cuts, sticking the wool to the skin with canvas tape.

'Will I be able to patrol tonight?' Arshad Ali asked from under the physician's hands.

'I would advise you to go home and get to bed. I'm sure your brother's men are perfectly capable of looking after us.'

As it evaporated the alcoholic content of the antiseptic solution began to numb the pain. Arshad Ali smiled. 'It's not that,' he said. 'We had planned a mahfil for tonight. A roast, hemp, cane liquor. And, of course, a whore.'

Dr Sharif glanced at the closed door behind which were his living quarters and spoke in a dropped voice: 'Isn't there enough of that sort of tamasha in this town already? My wife was in an uproar when she found out. And people here in the surgery have been talking of nothing else for the past fortnight.'

'I too have heard about the DC and his woman. Is she pretty?'

With difficulty Dr Sharif was cutting the hair growing around the wound in the upper lip. He stopped and looked deep into Arshad Ali's eyes. 'Don't worry about it,' he said, and after a moment's pause he added: 'Why don't your brothers find you a job? A nice consular post in Argentina, perhaps.'

Arshad Ali smiled again. 'Don't ruin my moustache, doctor-sahib.' The physician waited for the smile to fade, scissors suspended in air. 'My brothers were exactly the same at my age, doctor-sahib. The Ali seed is spread liberally throughout this region. Let me ask you something . . . it's a kind of joke. What happened to the man who once talked of sexual liberation? Tell me.'

Dr Sharif went over to the shelf to switch on the radio. The set, encased in dark mahogany with a cloth front, responded to the flick of the switch by emitting a grainy burst of melody. Dr Sharif lowered the volume and rotated the dial until he arrived at a frequency where someone was speaking in a foreign language. He consulted his wristwatch and came back to the couch.

Arshad Ali was waiting to complete his joke: 'His wife bore him a daughter.'

The voice on the radio stopped speaking, and after a few bars of music and a rapid succession of pips another voice said: 'This is the BBC World Service. Here is the news, read by—'

Dr Sharif lowered his head to the wounds.

The newscaster spoke in an impersonal voice: the monsoon floods in Bangladesh had been declared some of the worst in the region's history. Mark Tully, speaking over the sound of a torrent, expressed fears of a famine. Geography had made Bangladesh disaster-prone: most of the country was a giant river delta less than twenty feet above sea level, lying at the heart of a natural funnel formed by the Bay of Bengal. But the effects were magnified by poverty: in a nation where more than half the people were landless, the richly fertile silt islands that appeared and disappeared offshore were a great temptation – as soon as they built up, people paddled out to settle them.

Dr Sharif went to the other side of the room to close a window that was letting in insects. He fastened the bolt. Arshad Ali had closed his eyes – enjoying the cool alcohol on his face and inhaling its light vapour. Mark Tully came to the end of his report, and the newscaster moved on to the second story.

Arshad Ali opened his eyes and let out a whistle of disbelief. Dr Sharif rushed to the radio set and turned up the volume.

'A missile!' Arshad Ali gasped.

Dr Sharif raised a hand to quieten him and leaned in towards the radio. The General's plane had narrowly escaped a missile fired at it soon after take-off. The terrorist organisation allegedly led by the hanged prime minister's son was said to be responsible.

'A SAM-7,' said Dr Sharif, as though he knew what that was.

The newscaster moved on. Dr Sharif stood still for a few moments, hands dropped to his side, the open-beaked scissors clucking at the floor. Then he twisted the dial and arrived – through a series of high-pitched whistles, fragments of words and strains of music – at the national station. Here too news was under way.

'We'll have to wait for the summary at the end,' the physician said. They had obviously missed the lead item.

Working in silence the doctor finished dressing the wounds. Arshad Ali too listened intently. When the newscaster came to the end of the bulletin she repeated the headlines.

'I thought as much,' Dr Sharif said. 'They are not going to tell us about it.' He went to the shelf and turned off the radio with a savage twist.

'So,' Arshad Ali said. 'Nothing happened?'

'Obviously,' smiled Dr Sharif. 'As usual.' He put the remains of the gauze and the bottle of antiseptic in the curved dish and carried it to the desk. Frowning, he took the pen from his pocket and began writing on the note pad. 'The bandages will have to be changed every other day,' he said without looking up. 'And tomorrow' – he tore the page off the pad – 'send someone to the city to get these tetanus injections.'

Arshad Ali was standing up. 'In my stomach?' he joked and even managed to pull a face. But the doctor did not respond. He seemed eager to discuss the news with his wife.

Arshad Ali went to the door. The blood on his shirt was beginning to stiffen. Dr Sharif got up to let him out.

It was raining. Crickets sang. Darkness and silence pressed down on the huddled street; and for a brief confused moment Dr Sharif was unable to distinguish between the two. Then, filling his lungs with the warm humid air, he shouted after Arshad Ali: 'And make sure the chemist takes the injections out of a refrigerator.' A child had recently contracted polio in spite of the fact that she had been vaccinated. The heat had denatured the vaccine.

*Thursday*

—

The town awoke to the noisy heaving of the swollen rivers. A gigantic sweep of wind, rain and thunder had invaded the region during the night. The salt from the doorsteps was washed away and the rags stuffed in the drainpipes had to be taken out to drain the courtyards. Soon the houses were again full of the dancing water lizards. Screaming with rage servant girls all over the town drove clusters of them out of the downstairs rooms, only to find, moments later, even greater numbers entering the house through the gaps under the doors and through the drains.

The sky remained hidden behind thick clouds until noon when sunlight at last began to filter through. Mr Kasmi, immaculate in his starched and pressed attire, held the closed umbrella out of the front door and, releasing the catch, stepped on to the street. Other doors were being opened, too. Mr Kasmi covered the length of the street acknowledging and returning calls of greeting. He turned into the street that led to the school. The talli trees leaned over the pavement, dripping. In the far distance someone was walking towards him. Hidden somewhere in the tallis a papiha gave its mournful call. Mr Kasmi recognised the approaching figure as the newspaper photographer. His shoulders were hunched and his hands were thrust deep into the pockets of a large raincoat. The collar was turned up against the drizzle: Mr Kasmi liked the effect. The photographer saw Mr Kasmi and came to a stop under one of the trees.

'Saif Aziz has disappeared,' the man said, looking dejected, as Mr Kasmi came near. 'He's taken the car. His things aren't in the room and the hotel manager knows nothing.'

Mr Kasmi listened attentively. 'Perhaps he's gone back. It must have been an emergency,' he said. 'Maybe something to do with his family.'

155

'No.' The photographer took his hands out of the pockets. A piece of cottonwool was pressed to his forehead, held in place by two lengths of canvas tape that crossed each other at right angles. 'Haven't you heard about the attempt on the General's life?'

Mr Kasmi gave a nod.

'Saif's gone into hiding for fear of arrest.'

Mr Kasmi started to walk. 'Are you sure? Are you suggesting that he knew about it in advance.'

'No.' There was an edge to the photographer's voice. 'But there are bound to be repercussions. Anybody who has ever uttered a word against the regime is bound to be rounded up.'

'Perhaps,' said Mr Kasmi, 'he got a telegram saying one of the children is ill.'

'What telegram! There is no post office in this town.'

Mr Kasmi rounded his lips into an 'ah', remembering. 'Does the hotel have a telephone?'

The photographer shook his head slowly. They had drawn level with the optician's stall and began to cross the street. Sitting under the transparent canopy, the optician appeared to be engaged in a passionate discussion with the three men sitting with him on the bench. One of the men jabbed his finger furiously at the newspaper that lay folded in his lap and seemed to conclude his argument: 'It's a conspiracy!'

As Mr Kasmi and the photographer approached, all four men stood up respectfully to shake hands with the schoolteacher. 'What can I do for you, Kasmi-sahib?' asked the optician. The three men had remained standing.

'I was just on my way to . . .' Mr Kasmi pointed to the school-house fifty or so paces along the street. 'But has any of you seen the journalist this morning?'

The men shook their heads. One of them turned to the photographer and asked, 'Do you know anything about what happened last night?'

The photographer looked puzzled. 'I heard about it on Indian radio this morning. I am as much in the dark as you. There's nothing in the newspapers.'

'It's just international propaganda to weaken our country,' one of the men said forcefully. He was close to shouting. 'The General is a good man. Didn't he say that his civil servants should spend ten out of every thirty days living amongst ordinary people? If they don't obey him then it isn't his fault.'

A mocking smile – almost a sneer – played on the lips of the man with the newspaper. 'The man is an evil tyrant. Simple,' he said. 'Perhaps he should have gates put up at the ends of all the streets of the capital.'

The optician laughed. 'How about moats around the presidential palace. Just like in the days of the Mogul emperors.'

The jeers caused the General's supporter to shake his head in despair.

Mr Kasmi looked around. 'So,' he said quietly, 'you haven't seen him?' The group became suddenly serious. One man murmured a 'no'.

Mr Kasmi beckoned to the photographer and began to walk on. 'You should see Azhar about using his telephone. Try to get in touch with the offices of your paper and ask if they know why your friend has left.'

'I *know* why he's left,' the photographer grimaced.

Mr Kasmi nodded. 'If that is so then he must be a very honest man. He will have gone to prison under every government in the past thirty years.' At the end of the street they stopped. Mr Kasmi pointed along the side street and said, 'Turn left there. It's a small house with green doors and windows.'

The photographer took his handkerchief from his pocket and went down the street. Mr Kasmi too pressed his handkerchief to his nose. Fissures ran along the base of the school's outside wall. The surfaces were uneven, and water lizards – and most of the stench, Mr Kasmi supposed – escaped through these openings. A few sections of the wall leaned at dangerous angles while others had collapsed completely.

'Tarmac?' said the headmaster.

Mr Kasmi had come to propose a solution to the problem of the proliferating water lizards and the stench. 'Hot tarmac poured into the cracks will get rid of them.'

The headmaster heaved himself out of the chair and went to find the caretaker. Mr Kasmi looked around the office. On a shelf to the left of the headmaster's chair were two tarnished sports trophies. Above them on the wall were many black-and-white photographs of groups of students and teachers. Mr Kasmi appeared in a few. Directly above the chair was a large portrait of the Founder. And on the third wall, nailed around the window, there were framed ink drawings of the ancient buildings that had housed the first Islamic universities. These universities in Baghdad, Jerusalem, Cairo, Alexandria were a source of great pride throughout the Muslim world, despite the knowledge that most of these cities were famous as centres of learning long before the rise of Islam. The window was fringed on the outside by a trailing vine whose orange, trumpet-shaped flower, with its distinct stigma and stamens, had proved an indispensable visual aid to the science teacher who structured the biology course in such a way that the section dealing with plant reproduction always coincided with April.

The headmaster returned, accompanied by the caretaker – a hunched, torpid creature who, according to generations of students, had one glass eye. 'Nothing can be done till the rains stop,' he told Mr Kasmi. 'The boiling tarmac would have to be poured on dry earth. No use pouring it into mud.' He was holding his left hand flat and plunged his other hand on to it to demonstrate the act of pouring.

After the caretaker left, Mr Kasmi said, 'I suppose there'd be the same problem in trying to fill the holes with cement.'

The headmaster nodded. 'Nothing can be done till next spring.'

Mr Kasmi looked out through the open door: the door to the classroom across the corridor was shut. 'Not many students are attending school today, I suppose.'

'No.' The headmaster sat forward eagerly. 'How is this country

ever going to get ahead if a mere shower brings it to a standstill?'
He seemed to adopt, Mr Kasmi noticed, the attitude which he
employed during the morning assembly. 'It wouldn't happen
anywhere else in the world. People in other countries go to work
despite the rains. Even in snow. Here shops are closed and people
idle about at home.'

Mr Kasmi picked up his bag. He hesitated before he spoke.
'It's not as simple as that. If you have only one pair of shoes and
can only afford one set of presentable clothes then it is advisable
to stay at home during the rains and not get them muddied.
Have you seen the state of the streets?'

'Excuses, excuses, Kasmi-sahib.'

'Things *are* changing, but it will take time. Remember the
school at the beginning? Now it's bigger and has more teachers.
We have to be patient.'

'No. If the school is bigger it's because someone has worked for
it. I went and stood at every door, asking for donations, ceiling
fans, anything. It would not have expanded if, as you suggest, we
had just waited.'

'I didn't suggest that,' Mr Kasmi said, 'I just think we should
be tolerant.' He was standing up.

A square packet stood on the floor by the headmaster's desk.
Part of its brown wrapper had been torn to reveal the contents:
a row of identical books, each the size of an address book,
no more than a few inches in length, and bound in a beautiful
green.

The headmaster said, 'Bad habits have to be criticised, Kasmi-
sahib. Otherwise nothing will change.' He registered Mr Kasmi's
glance at the packet of books and bent down to take one out
through the opening in the wrapper. 'They arrived on Monday.
The parcel was one of the things in the lost mail-bag.' He passed
the book to Mr Kasmi.

'The Little Green Book,' Mr Kasmi read aloud the words
embossed in goldleaf on the brow of the book. He opened it. It
was a book commissioned by the country's first chief martial-
law administrator and contained 'the President's thoughts'.

Copies of it had been sent to schools, mosques, cinema houses, hotels, roadside tea-stalls and, it was said at the time, to brothels.

Mr Kasmi was shaking his head. 'It was . . .' he struggled, 'how many years ago?'

'Nineteen. The gold leaf is still incredibly shiny though.'

Mr Kasmi closed the book.

'Take it,' the headmaster offered. 'I don't know what to do with them.'

Mr Kasmi unzipped his bag and placed the book inside. 'Perhaps we should try to block the holes with them.'

His words were choked by the gust of foul smell that rose to meet him from below.

Azhar held the cigarette in his mouth, his lips curling around the yellow filter, and lowered his head to the flame. He inhaled the smoke deep into his body and letting the matchstick fall on to the marble floor stepped on it without looking down.

'I still don't know what to do about the post office,' he said. 'There's no sign of the postmaster.'

Mujeeb Ali said, 'It'll be hard to find him now. What with this thing last night about the General. He won't come out into the daylight for a long while yet.'

Azhar nodded. 'I haven't received the list yet but I'm sure his name will be near the top.' The words were muffled by the thick blue smoke he exhaled. The smoke floated out of the open window, towards the twisting river.

'They say it was the work of the secessionists from Baluchistan,' Mujeeb Ali said companionably.

'Secessionists? What secessionists?' Azhar feigned surprise. 'That region is at peace, remember. No civil war is raging in that region.'

A worn smile spread across Mujeeb Ali's face.

'Lahore is under curfew,' Azhar said.

Mujeeb Ali said: 'How is everything in Lahore? Sabina and the children?'

Azhar did not look up. 'They are very well.' And then he said: 'I heard about your visit to Elizabeth.'

The dark skin under Mujeeb Ali's eyes had tightened. 'You cannot go on living this way. Either get rid of her or marry her. The current set-up is not right because people have found out.'

The younger man shut his eyes and nodded that he understood.

'Why so much fuss over a chodhi? Get rid of her to stop people talking.'

Azhar nodded. 'We'll see.'

※

Benjamin Massih sat up. He had spent most of the previous two weeks lying in bed with a dislocated elbow and a broken shin-bone. The masseur had aligned the broken bone and reengaged the joint. Schoolboys' wooden rulers had been used as splints. A little dazed, he gently lowered his feet to the earthen floor. He stood up, and sat down almost immediately. He looked around the narrow low-ceilinged room. Two rope cots were set against the opposite wall. A large crucifix was hanging from a rusty nail driven deep into the mud wall, deep into the wooden frame of the house. A shelf, trimmed with zigzags of newspaper, held a framed religious print: the gold leaf was flaky and the scarlet had faded to a dull pink. Benjamin stood up again, more care-fully, and through the open door of the room looked out at the courtyard edged with pots of herbs. He walked stiffly to the door and, once there, called: 'Tereza.'

His wife came out of the kitchen and was alarmed at seeing him out of bed. 'Get back on to the cot.'

Benjamin Massih had turned around and was dragging his left leg behind him like a lame animal. 'I'm hungry,' he said without turning around.

Tereza Massih was at his side. 'You shouldn't be moving your limbs yet.' Around her neck she wore a silver chain on which hung a tiny Jesus Christ – arms outstretched, legs lightly bowed at the knees. There was no cross behind the figure – it was almost as though the wearer herself was the cross on to which the Messiah was nailed.

Benjamin Massih smiled. 'I know you're trying to starve me to death. I wouldn't be surprised to find that you've sent for Father Emmanuel to give me Extreme Unction.'

Tereza Massih smiled. 'You shouldn't have got up.' She helped Benjamin Massih back into bed, doubled the pillow and arranged it behind the invalid's spine. 'I'll bring some soup.' Her flaxen hair was gathered at the nape of the neck with a rag.

'What is it?' Benjamin Massih asked when she returned to the room bearing a clay bowl.

'Trotters.' The woman set the bowl on the floor and went back into the kitchen for a spoon and a low stool of unplaned wood.

'Nothing tastes the way it used to once,' Benjamin Massih lamented as his wife fed him the first spoonful. The room was full of mosquitoes. The small window admitted the noise of running water and the smell of dung.

Tereza Massih dipped the brass spoon in the bowl and inhaled the warm vapour that pirouetted delicately on the surface of the soup before rising up. 'Age has mangled our taste-buds.' She lifted the spoon to the open mouth.

But later – the soup half gone – Benjamin Massih smacked his lips. 'Trotters make the tastiest soup.'

His wife nodded in agreement.

'And sheep's tail, too,' he said, swallowing.

'Do you remember what your father-ji, may he rest in peace, used to call a sheep's tail?'

'Arse lid,' the man said promptly, and laughed, invigorated by the food.

The woman tried to contain her laughter. 'Some people say you can make soup from chicken claws too.'

'Yes,' said Benjamin Massih. 'I have tasted it. Very tasty with a day-old tandoori naan.'

She grimaced. The soup was finished; she tilted the bowl and coaxed the last murky mouthful into the spoon.

'Some people eat brain and eyeballs. Rich people!' Benjamin Massih swallowed the last, slightly too salty, mouthful. He was enjoying the distaste on his wife's face.

She was standing up. 'Stop right there, Benjamin Massih,' she said through a smile; she was giving him a fake reproving look. 'I *know* which part of the body you're going to mention next.' She picked up the stool – the Messiah swung back and forth between her chest and chin – and went to the door.

Benjamin Massih was laughing stridently now. 'And, of course, people eat sheep's testicles,' he shouted after her. He heard her laugh in the small kitchen next door. He wiped his lips on his sleeve, unfolded the pillow and, still smiling hugely, lowered his head on to the pillow.

Some minutes later he heard her call out: 'Stay where you are.'

He raised his head and caught a glimpse of her crossing the courtyard. Someone was at the door. Their door always stood open; a tattered hessian curtain was all that prevented sight of the courtyard from the street. He could hear the woman attending to the caller.

'Are you Elizabeth Massih's mother?'

'Yes.'

Maulana Hafeez folded his umbrella. His face was chafed by the winds that had risen during the evening. He smiled politely: 'I would like to talk to your husband.'

'Who are you?' Tereza Massih had pulled her stole over her hennaed hair.

'Hadji Maulana Hafeez Bux Bukhari.'

The woman understood immediately. She looked around and, her fingers furiously gripping the edge of the door, invited Maulana Hafeez into the house.

She let down one of the cots and gestured Maulana Hafeez to sit. Then she helped Benjamin Massih to sit up.

Maulana Hafeez asked about the injuries. While her husband talked, Tereza Massih switched on the light bulb that hung from a hook in the centre of the ceiling. The light reached every corner of the room, like spilt sugar. Tereza Massih closed the window and lighted a mosquito-repellent coil. Despite her silence she seemed poised, alert.

'It's about your daughter Elizabeth,' Maulana Hafeez said at last.

'What about her?' Benjamin Massih gave a nod.

Maulana Hafeez's fingers felt along the rosary. 'How old is she?'

'She says she's twenty-one but she's older,' said Benjamin Massih. Maulana Hafeez took a deep breath. Tereza Massih left the room and went into the corrugated-iron shack that served as the kitchen. There was no electricity there: as she entered, a draught disturbed the flame of the candle and the diffused shadows cast on the walls swayed.

'Are you aware that she's living with someone outside of wedlock?' Maulana Hafeez realised that his fingers were trembling.

'Yes,' Benjamin Massih said in a discomforted tone.

Maulana Hafeez felt lost, at sea. 'I have to believe that I'm doing the right thing,' he began at random. 'Otherwise I've wasted my whole life and—'

'How does that concern us?'

'They have to get married,' Maulana Hafeez said abruptly.

'They can't,' replied Benjamin Massih. 'He's a Muslim and she's a Roman Catholic.'

'She has to convert.'

'One of them has to.'

Maulana Hafeez stood up; that a Muslim should change his religion was inconceivable. 'I have not read your holy book—'

'The Bible.'

'The Bible,' Maulana Hafeez said. 'But I know that it too condemns this sort of behaviour.'

'Look, sahib,' Benjamin Massih said, 'I was explaining this earlier to the other Muslim priest who came to see me about Elizabeth: I'm a church-going man, I'm ashamed of what she's doing, I can't look anyone in the face, I'm glad I'm bedridden so that I don't have to leave the house. But what can I do? What could I possibly do? It's all up to them.'

Maulana Hafeez sat down. 'Nothing is that simple. Since they live among other people they have a responsibility, a moral obligation, towards those people. We *must* make them see this. They cannot ignore the wishes of the rest of us and still continue to live among us.'

'I have talked to her but she won't listen.'

Maulana Hafeez sighed. 'They are foolishly proud. It is a fruitless rebellion.'

The icy blue smoke of the fumigation coil was filling up the room and the drone of the mosquitoes had faded.

Tereza Massih came in from the kitchen with a cup for the Muslim priest.

'Your daughter has to convert,' Maulana Hafeez appealed to her as she bent down to offer the tea.

'I won't allow it,' she said. She had gone to sit by her husband's side. 'She'll remain a Roman Catholic till the day she dies.' And pointing to the tea she said: 'The cup has been washed, sahib.'

Maulana Hafeez nodded. He raised the cup to his lips and took a sip.

*Mother and Father sit in the circle of light. He is eating rice and tindé. Above them, attracted by the smell of Kala-Kola hair tonic, clusters of mosquitoes whine, their paths a mess of tangles and knots.*

*Father says, 'Don't send her to work tomorrow.'*

*'She was crying when she came back'.*

*'They'll send someone to ask after her, and then you can talk to them about it.'*

*'What if no one comes?'*

*'They'll come. She has always been good with their little boy. He has grown to love her, you told me that.'*

*The lamp hangs from the hook, swaying. Their shadows go round in circles. I change sides and Mother looks towards my cot.*

*She lowers her voice. 'The boy's uncle hit her and the mother pulled her hair.'*

*'Well, when they send someone to fetch her you can talk to them. They are good people. They gave her new clothes for Eid.'*

*'And we need the money she brings in.'*

*He nods. Inside its glass bubble, the flame is like the bud of a yellow rose. Father says, 'And you must ask her to be more careful, too. They hire her to mind their little boy. It's her job to look after him properly.'*

*Mother gives a nod. 'She says she only left him unattended for a second. A new toy vendor had come into the street and all the girls had gone to look at the things.'*

*'Is the little boy badly hurt?'*

*'They've taken him to hospital.'*

*'Well, when they send someone round to ask why she hasn't showed up for work, you can talk to them. Tell them they're not to slap her again, no matter what she does. If they have a complaint they should come to us. She's just a child herself.'*

*I close my eyes, and try to sleep.*

*Friday*

—

The rain was so fierce that water from the eaves fell in continuous threads, like a beaded curtain. Alice was on the veranda pounding cinnamon in a mortar, her face tensed with effort as she brought down the pestle. Her knees were splayed out and the mortar was clamped between the undersides of her feet. She changed arms when she tired, or began to grind in a circular motion instead of pounding. And all the while she talked chirpily. Zébun sat on the rope cot and listened. Occasionally she nodded, causing her gold earrings to swing towards her cheeks. To ease the burden on her earlobes the heavy earrings were supported by lengths of black thread attached to the hairpins.

Alice was describing a recent visit to the cinema. 'And then a baby started crying in the audience, so loud you couldn't hear anything. After a while, from near the front, a man shouted, Shove a tit in its mouth, sister.' She gave a broad laugh. But Zébun merely nodded. Alice lingered a moment and then began to pound the spices again.

'It doesn't feel like a Friday,' Zébun said. Alice stopped; looked up for a moment, like a deer at a water-hole, and then set to again. It was a long and empty morning. The sky loomed dead above the courtyard. The jasmine bush cresting the far wall swayed in the rain, doors creaked, window panes rattled in the frames and curtains swelled into the rooms like ship sails. Above them, from one wall of the veranda to the other, clothes were drying. Zébun's underclothes were concealed beneath other, neutral clothes, or beneath towels and sheets, away from Mr Kasmi's eyes. An unbroken line of salt ran along the edge of the veranda like a miniature mountain range.

When some time later Alice mentioned the goat with the sacred markings Zébun said, 'I would like to see it. Though I don't think they'll let me into the house.'

Alice looked up at her mistress hesitantly. 'It's nothing,' she waved a hand consolingly. 'We too have something like that in our religion.' And she explained how the darker hair growing along a donkey's back and down part of the front legs was said to describe a crucifix. 'They say it's because Jesus Christ, our prophet, made the journey from Jerusalem on a donkey's back.'

Zébun understood that the story was meant as an expression of sympathy, and appreciated it. She smiled. Splashing rainwater was gouging away the outer side of the salt line making tiny irregular cliffs. Zébun pointed and said, 'You'd better go into the kitchen and get some more salt, or you'll have to spend the rest of the day driving water lizards out of the house.'

Alice nodded and stood up purposefully.

Zébun said, 'And when the rain is over remind me to give you a letter to post.'

'The post office is still shut,' the girl said. Above the neck-line of her shirt her sharp little collar-bone stuck out, fantastically exaggerated.

'Then I'd better ask brother-ji for advice.' Zébun considered the stairs leading up to Mr Kasmi's room. 'Has he arisen?'

Alice nodded, 'I heard music from upstairs a while ago. But he hasn't been down for breakfast yet.'

The sergeant lowered the book he was reading. The chair was tipped back on two legs. On the wall where his head rested the plaster was worn and grimy. He brought down the chair and, sighing, pressed the book to his chest where Wamaq Saleem's signature was tattooed. 'How can they let us have his books for money alone?' He left the chair and went to stand in the doorway. Above the door hung a framed document, listing the ten qualities – each expressed by an adjective – considered to be the essence of an ideal policeman.

The police inspector was reading the newspaper. 'Were you patrolling last night?' he asked from behind the paper.

Mosquitoes cruised around the room, silently for the most part; only occasionally was the keening of a female to be heard. The floor was caked with mud brought in on people's shoes. 'No. It was my turn as barracks orderly.' He smiled: 'I did patrol the night before last, though.'

The tone of voice had betrayed the smile: the inspector lowered the newspaper and looked at the sergeant.

The sergeant brought his foot down on a water lizard then, without looking, sent the creature flying with an economical kick. It landed on its ribbed back, split from end to end and scraping the air uselessly with its legs like a wind-up toy that has been knocked over.

Mr Kasmi was at the other side of the courthouse, nimbly stepping around the puddles. The sergeant had seen Mr Kasmi often enough before on his way to Yusuf Rao's office. But today was Friday, and the sergeant realised that Mr Kasmi was walking towards the barracks.

'It's about the post office,' Mr Kasmi said. 'I would like to know how long the postal system in this town is to remain in paralysis. I have a letter to post.'

The police inspector leaned forward and rested his hands on the desktop, fingers slatted into each other. 'It won't be long, Kasmi-sahib. I think by the middle of next week the DC will have informed the central post office of the vacancy. And soon after that the new postmaster should arrive.'

The sergeant had gone back to his chair. He was hanging on the insistent drone of a mosquito. He followed the insect's erratic flight, his eyes doodling, and when the whine stopped he stiffened and smacked his forearm. There was a smear of blood on the skin. 'What a waste,' he grinned. 'My own blood.'

The inspector smiled. 'Have it tattooed in.'

His subordinate smiled back. Then he got to his feet and

brought his book to Mr Kasmi, a forefinger pressed firmly into the page. 'What does this word mean, Kasmi-sahib?'

Mr Kasmi raised a finger in the air. 'It's a Persian word.' He told the sergeant what the word meant. 'When Wamaq Saleem began writing poetry, in his student days, he didn't know any Persian. That, of course, was a great disadvantage since our language draws so heavily from Persian. So he had to learn it.'

The sergeant, nodding vigorously, went back to his chair.

Mr Kasmi cleared his throat and turned to the police inspector. 'And what are we citizens supposed to do until then?'

The inspector scratched his head. 'Leave the letter with me, Kasmi-sahib. I'll have it sent to the city.'

'I don't understand why the post office is shut, anyway,' Mr Kasmi said. 'The postmaster may have gone missing but the post*man* is still here. Why not get him to take charge until a new postmaster can be appointed?' And he said to himself: 'I'll suggest this to Azhar.'

The police inspector allowed a little irritation in his voice. 'You'll have to wait till the end of next week, Kasmi-sahib. The DC'll be away for some time. Ever since the attempt on the General's life there have been emergency meetings everywhere.'

Mr Kasmi nodded.

'I myself was away all day yesterday,' said the police inspector. 'There are plans now to enlarge the barracks. More men and a larger lock-up. It will be a proper police station.' There was pride in his voice. At that he let the matter drop and exclaimed: 'Where are my manners? Would you like a cup of tea, Kasmi-sahib?' And ignoring Mr Kasmi's refusal, he clicked his fingers at the sergeant; but he was already rushing to the tea-stall across the street.

❧

The loudspeaker of the mosque growled, frightening away the papihas, and after the prolonged note of the feedback-whistle, a male voice began to recite verses from the Qur'an.

Yusuf Rao's twelve-year-old son sat cross-legged on the floor cleaning his father's weekday shoes. He had taken out the laces and was using the handle of a spoon to prise out rectangles of caked mud from the pattern on the sole. From the courtyard high-pitched yelps and urgent commands – sound of his brothers and sisters at play – reached the room. Yusuf Rao was at the other side of the room engaged in a conversation with Mr Kasmi. The Little Green Book was on the table by Yusuf Rao's elbow.

Mr Kasmi said, 'I think you should lie low for a while.'

Yusuf Rao picked up the Little Green Book; he held it in his hand for a moment before returning it to the table. 'They won't come for me. I think they know that I gave all that up years ago.'

'But there's no harm in being careful,' Mr Kasmi said in his precise way. 'Did you hear about Saif Aziz?'

'Yes,' Yusuf Rao replied. 'I think he was very wise. I would've done the same if I was still active. The repression's bound to increase.' He broke off and, a smile on his face, asked: 'Did Saif Aziz tell you how Mujeeb Ali's brother, after he became a minister, tried to buy him? No? Well, he sent a brand new Volkswagen round to his house with a note saying, It's a gift, I know it's your favourite car. Saif Aziz sent it back saying, My *favourite* car is a Mercedes-Benz; a Volkswagen is what I can *afford*.'

Mr Kasmi smiled. 'Did he get a Mercedes-Benz?'

Yusuf Rao made a theatrical sour face. 'Much cheaper to shut the whole paper down.'

Yusuf Rao's youngest daughter entered the room. She wore a bright blue frock and her long straight hair was gathered with a ribbon; the fringe was held away from the forehead with a dragonfly hair-clip. She was holding a large peepul leaf in her hand. Mr Kasmi lifed her on to his lap and began skilfully to fold the supple leaf.

'I wonder who fired the missile?' Mr Kasmi said.

'The BBC said it was the hanged prime minister's son. But according to the All India Radio it was the guerrillas from Baluchistan,' said Yusuf Rao. And he added grimly: 'I don't envy whoever comes to power in the wake of this regime.'

Mr Kasmi almost interrupted him. 'I wish we could find out who actually runs this country. The army? The politicians? The industrialists? The landowners?' He had stopped work on the peepul leaf to say this: the little girl poked him in the ribs, prompting him to continue.

Yusuf Rao smiled and referred to the voices from the mosques. 'Or is it God?'

The boy had wiped the mud off the shoes and was about to begin polishing them. 'No,' Yusuf Rao said across the room. 'The smell gives me a headache. Take them somewhere else.'

The boy sighed with annoyance and left the room. Mr Kasmi pointed to the mud he left behind and made a comment about the weather.

When the leaf had been securely folded into a whistle, Mr Kasmi held one end of the neat package between his lips and gently breathed into it: there was free passage of air. The child was already on her feet. She muttered a word of thanks when the whistle was handed to her, and blew into it immediately. The sharp rasping noise startled the adults. Mr Kasmi looked abashed. She went out with skipping steps, her eyes glowing with delight.

Yusuf Rao's wife brought in the coffee. Her hair was wet and hung limply on either side of her face, each strand ending in a large drop of water. She smelled of clean water. 'You should stay for lunch, brother-ji,' she said to Mr Kasmi. 'But it will be late. It's Friday so I had to have a bath.' She handed them their cups. 'I don't know how you can drink this. It smells of chick-pea sauce that's been left on the stove for too long.'

Mr Kasmi said, 'You may be right, sister-ji. Coffee *is* a kind of roasted bean.'

Yusuf Rao said noisily, 'I drink it because it reminds me of my student days.' He winked at his wife.

'You have no shame, Yusuf Rao,' the woman said, smiling. And she turned to Mr Kasmi: 'Your friend has no shame, brother-ji.'

Yusuf Rao sipped the drink. He said, 'Your brother-ji was just telling me that they're planning a bigger police station for this town. More men and a bigger building, perhaps a promotion for the inspector. I think that's proof enough that something *did* happen on Wednesday night.'

The woman sought Mr Kasmi's eyes. He nodded.

'The sooner we get rid of this evil general, the better,' she said. She turned to Yusuf Rao and said: 'When the government changes I'm going to make a list of all the things you once did for the opposition and I'm going to get you a ministership.'

'I've given up all that.'

There was bitter resentment in the woman's voice. 'They accused our party of electoral fraud. But in this town it was Mujeeb Ali who rigged the ballots.'

'Nation-wide it was us,' Yusuf Rao said. 'And that's what counts. Everyone cheats, so the one who cheats the most *is* the cheater. But why dig it all up again? As I said, I gave up on all that years ago. I don't want to be a minister, bibi. The boys will be grown up in a few years. They'll start earning.'

'They'll disappoint me yet.' The woman went to the door. 'Fridays drive me insane. Children are home, husband is home and, on top of that, there's this noise from the mosques.'

'What did the poor *husband* do?' Yusuf Rao shouted after her.

By three o'clock, when they sat down to eat, the prayers had been said at both mosques. Maulana Dawood had finished his sermon; Maulana Hafeez was just beginning his.

There was bésan stew with dumplings, tur salad – almost out of season now – and iced lemon water. Dessert would be pistachio halva which everyone knew smelled better than it tasted. Yusuf Rao's wife and eldest daughter – the pair had said their prayers – laid the table. One of the boys was attempting from memory Charlie Chaplin's bread-roll dance with two spoons; the children had seen the film from which the sequence came on the television the night before. The eldest girl began to make chappatis. Her mother served the food.

Maulana Hafeez's voice carried through the streets. *And what if the entire world has wandered down the wrong path? We must still fight to keep ourselves pure. Remember that the darkness which*

175

*has the ability to overpower a mountain is beaten by the tiniest of flames.*

They ate in silence. The peepul-leaf whistle, clogged now with saliva, was next to the little girl's plate. Yusuf Rao's wife took away the stew dish and returned with it filled to the brim leaving a trail of steam behind her. She was listening to Maulana Hafeez without blinking.

The cleric was easing into his sermon. *We have forgotten what lies in store for sinners. A flame that is a thousand times more poisonous than any fire of this earth.*

The twelve-year-old spent his time at the table pulling down his sleeve to cover a shoe-polish stain on his wrist. The little girl knocked over a glass of water.

Maulana Hafeez spoke for another ten minutes, his voice rising as, for the first time, he openly condemned the deputy commissioner and his mistress. *Ties of family, friendship and faith keep us united against the attentions of Shaitan.*

One by one the children left the table; no one managed to finish dessert. Mr Kasmi pressed his handkerchief to his lips. Yusuf Rao belched. The girl shouted from the kitchen to know how many chappatis were left. She slid the baking-iron under the shelf. Mother and daughter cleared the table, wiped down the surface and sat down to eat. Beads of sweat glistened on the girl's brow.

It was many minutes before anyone spoke.

'It seems that Maulana Hafeez is turning into a Maulana Dawood,' Yusuf Rao said.

'Maulana-ji is right,' his wife said. 'Somebody had to speak out. Those two are behaving like pigs. Now they'll have to take notice and do the decent thing.' Her breathing was laboured but her tone was measured, careful not to embarrass the girl in front of her father or make the father uncomfortable by being open with him in front of the daughter; and, of course, there was Mr Kasmi.

The heavy meal and the heat were combining to induce a stupor. Yusuf Rao fingered the collar of his shirt, and said, 'He didn't have to mention them by name though.'

Mr Kasmi took a breath. 'What difference does that make? Everyone would have known who was being referred to anyway.'

Gul-kalam's family had gone back to their village in the mountains. Their house – the lubinium just coming into leaf – stood locked. They had taken the morning bus out of town. The compact little group had been ignored by everyone who passed by the bus station. Kalsum and Suraya watched them through the window as they came down the back lane and turned the corner – the women with jewels in the ridge between their nostrils, the half-asleep children and the wide-awake babies, the crippled brother, the goats, the heavy trunks and bundles. Suraya had said, closing the window, 'There was no need for them to leave.'

Now Kalsum and Suraya sat on the veranda. There was no wind, hardly a breeze. Leaves whispered on the arbour.

'What did Yusuf Rao say when you went to see him yesterday?' Kalsum asked.

'He says if Burkat wants me to divorce him then I should keep the house,' Suraya said.

'And put him out?'

'Yes.'

Kalsum lifted an eyebrow. 'Where would he go?'

'What do I care!'

'For shame!' Kalsum touched her earlobes. 'Such talk from a Muslim. He's your *husband* . . . And what about the boy?'

Suraya's eyes softened. 'He says I have a right to him as well.' Her face had lit up at the mention of her son. 'He's tall, apa. Two hands taller than his father. Only fourteen years old.' Good food and a healthy environment had unlocked the information in the boy's genes; information that had been dormant in his father and uncles.

'So,' Kalsum said, 'you've decided to go back.'

Suraya did not reply. Instead, she said: 'You'd be alone here if I go, apa. Once again.'

Kalsum folded her arms. 'Don't worry about me. I'm happy where my men have left me.'

The sunlight yellowed, turned amber and then faded.

The barber locked the door to his shop and jumped down from the platform. He and Zafri walked together towards their homes. They lived in the same lane by the western river. They kept silent as they passed Judge Anwar's house. A cat jumped down from a tree and crossed their path.

Inside Judge Anwar's house the youngest girl took the chewed toffee out of her mouth to see what colour it had become. One of her sisters – her eyes swollen from ten days of tears – rebuked her. The child scuttled out of the room, blowing bubbles with the warm saliva thick with caramel. The widow listened to a noise for some minutes before realising that it was the sound of her own breathing. There was a flash of lightning. The widow smiled acquiescently at the child who had just come into the room and said: 'God's taking a picture.'

Most of the town was dipped in darkness. Wavering spheres of street light, speckled with drizzle, floated above the streets. Tereza Massih crossed herself and closed the window. She lighted a fumigation coil. Benjamin Massih murmured something in his sleep which she strained to catch. She picked up the plate containing the crusty edges of a chappati and went out.

Two blocks away Dr Sharif twisted the dial of the radio. The needle sliced across a station where a melancholy song was being played. The physician returned to the song and remained immersed in its lulling sentiment long after it had faded.

Mr Kasmi got ready to walk the four blocks to Mujeeb Ali's house. He collected his umbrella and turned off the bedroom light. As he descended the stairs his shadow trailed behind him like an emperor's robe. Downstairs Alice felt the day's washing: it was still damp and would have to be left out on the veranda overnight. Mr Kasmi arrived at the bottom of the staircase and called, 'Ready?' He was to walk Alice home before going to Mujeeb Ali's house to give his daughters their private lesson.

'Where's Arshad?' said Nabila Ali, pushing aside the embroidered mosquito-netting and addressing the cook who had come to the bedroom door to take her leave. She was taking home the day's left-over food. She shrugged but answered all the same, 'He's gone to have his bandages changed.' Nabila Ali nodded: 'Has Kasmi-sahib's tea been sent in?' The cook nodded and left.

By nine o'clock the drizzle was coalescing into heavy rain. Elizabeth was on her way to the bedroom when she heard the knock. 'Who is it?' she said and went towards the door. She was answered by another knock much louder than the first. Elizabeth stopped in the centre of the courtyard and raised a hand to her chest. She was without her veil. She had heard Maulana Hafeez's sermon today and had decided that from now on she would always cover her head before answering the door. As she turned, the knock came again, but so sharply that a little scream escaped her lips. 'He's not in,' she shouted. Then she took several paces away from the door, which was being pushed from the street, violently. She could make out shouts above the sound of the raindrops. 'He's not here,' she said, or thought, as the door swung through a complete half-circle and hit the wall.

Thunder rolled across the sky. Maulana Hafeez read the appropriate verse. He switched off the mosque lights one by one, fastened the street door and went into the house. He coughed as he crossed the veranda and had to stand still for a moment to get his breath back. 'I didn't see the newspaper today,' he said as he

179

entered the kitchen. His wife removed the milk from the fire but it continued to boil, absorbing heat from the sides of the pan. She blew into the froth. 'They say the streets of all the big cities are crawling with army vehicles. The newspaper photographer phoned his office today, that's how everyone knows.' Maulana Hafeez shook his head. 'God is merciful.' The woman had got up and was standing at the window to the street. 'Something's happening outside, Maulana-ji,' she said; her small, frail body was alert. Maulana Hafeez stood up. 'Listen, Maulana-ji. I can hear shouting.'

*Saturday*

—

At last, Maulana Hafeez rose. He yawned indulgently like a child, his jaw askew, read the appropriate verse, and cupped his profile in the soft palms of his hands – a solemn gesture of gratitude towards the Creator for granting him one more day. He had awakened not long after falling asleep and had spent a restless few hours lying on his back, listening to the rain.

He took down the hurricane lamp hanging from the door-frame and carried it to the other end of the room. There he raised the glass globe by pressing the lever and lighted the wick. Then Maulana Hafeez took out the clothes hanging in the wardrobe and began to dress.

Running his tongue over his gums he collected the stale saliva, thick with the vapours from his stomach, and went to the window. He opened the casements and spat the putrid matter out into the darkness. Despite the eaves above the window a violent rush of wind drenched his face with rain. The town resounded beneath the downpour. From a tree in a distant courtyard a papiha's reedy cry reached the bedroom. Monsoon, Maulana Hafeez thought, and closed the window.

Without noticing the hour he wound the clock with its rusty moth-like key. The alarm went off in his hands. It was five minutes to four o'clock. Maulana Hafeez remembered that on the night of Judge Anwar's murder, he had got up to say the pre-dawn prayers twenty-five minutes earlier. Winter was drawing close. For a brief moment he thought he heard Gul-kalam blow his whistle, as he had done on many other nights over the years.

Guided by the light of the lamp – the electricity had failed around midnight – the cleric crossed the veranda to the toilet. Ten minutes later he emerged exhausted, and glanced at his wife's bedroom. The door was open.

In the kitchen the fire had settled into languid flames with blunt tips. Maulana Hafeez's wife poured him a cup of tea. 'What is going to happen when Azhar comes back?' she asked quietly.

Maulana Hafeez was precise. 'The girl will have to change her religion and they'll get married. I'll make them see sense.' He meant to say more but, seized by a coughing attack, could not continue. He had a chill on his chest and his legs and back were stiff from lying motionless like a corpse for so many hours.

The woman set her hand on his wrist and felt for fever. 'Don't go to the mosque this morning, Maulana-ji,' she said. 'Rafiq Asan can lead the prayers today. You need to rest.'

Maulana Hafeez shook his head. 'I have to go. Especially today.'

He finished his tea in silence. Swallowing the last sweet gulp, he leaned towards the fire to look for the chip of cinnamon at the bottom of the cup. The release of the oily resin in his mouth comforted him.

In the bathroom, after he had performed his ablutions and was about to unbolt the door, Maulana Hafeez began to weep. Blind with tears he leaned against the door and remained there for many minutes. Then, even though tears did not annul an ablution, he performed the consoling ritual once more.

The woman heard him gargle as she looked for his white cap. Last night she had stretched the wet cap over the base of an upturned bowl. She carried the bowl surmounted by the cap to the kitchen door.

She murmured something but Maulana Hafeez raised a hand. He took the dry cap and arranged it on his head. He felt in his pocket for the keys to the mosque.

Mr Kasmi pushed the tip of the scissors into the cocoon and cut around the silky sphere. The hollow case, acting as sounding-board, amplified the noise of the blades. Mr Kasmi pulled the two halves apart – the brittle curved body of the silkworm dropped on to the table. He ran a forefinger inside each half of the cocoon, blew, and placed them in the pan with the other ingredients. Next, he picked up a large dried berry and examined the skin for holes ants might have made to lay their eggs in. He peeled the berry and threw both the skin and the stone into the pan. He completed the recipe of the infusion by adding a few dried petals of the kuchnar blossom. The original pink had deepened to lilac. Each spring Alice would look greedily at the tree laden with buds. 'We should pluck them all and cook them before they become flowers; they're really delicious,' she never tired of saying. Zébun would retort: 'I had the tree planted for its flowers; we can get the buds for cooking from the vegetable man.' And the servant girl, pulling a face in deep irritation: 'It seems such a waste; and it isn't too high for me to climb either; Kasmi-sahib could hold the ladder steady.'

A smile came to Mr Kasmi's lips. 'Our Alice-bibi isn't here yet,' he thought out loud.

Zébun read a verse, kept count by letting slide a bead along the thread, and said, 'I don't think she'll come today, brother-ji. The Christians won't let their girls out for a long while yet.'

Mr Kasmi surfaced. 'Yes,' he said vaguely.

Zébun lowered the rosary. 'Men are worse than animals. Janvar!'

'It wasn't just men who did that thing last night, sister-ji. There were women there, too. And children.'

Zébun watched Mr Kasmi anxiously, her shoulders bent forward. 'You *are* unhurt, aren't you, brother-ji?'

'I was unhurt,' Mr Kasmi lied.

Zébun nodded.

'I was just knocked to the ground. But Maulana Hafeez placed himself between me and the crowd just in time.'

'Your voice sounds different,' Zébun said, 'but this' – she gestured towards the pan on the fire – 'should stop you catching pneumonia. At our age we mustn't let night rain on to our lungs.'

Mr Kasmi smiled in accord and looked into the pan. Even though the water was only just warming up, a microscopic imperfection in the surface of the metal was assisting the process of oxidation and a column of tiny bubbles was rising from the base of the pan to the surface.

'You were very courageous, brother-ji.' Zébun shook her head. 'I would have continued walking.'

'It wasn't deliberate, sister-ji. It was all so very sudden. And, I must admit that afterwards I did feel a little foolish. All I remember is that on my way back from Mujeeb Ali I saw the girl being dragged through the street. And the next thing I know I've crossed the street and am struggling with these people. Then a section of the crowd turns on *me*: Get the Ahmadiya as well. Get the Ahmadiya as well.'

'And that's when Maulana Hafeez arrived?'

'It must have been.'

A wisp of steam was rising and the water was beginning to boil, diminishing in volume – a ball of wool being unwound by the drawing out of the loose end.

Mr Kasmi continued: 'The front end of the crowd kept on moving forward so eventually we were left alone in the street, Maulana Hafeez and I. Maulana Hafeez was trying to get me back on my feet. And someone near the back of the mob shouted to him: "Maulana-ji, you wouldn't see Maulana Dawood associating so freely with an Ahmadiya." '

Mr Kasmi finished speaking with a little catarrhal laugh.

The sound appeared to bring Zébun out of a daydream.

Outside, the morning was calm – clouded heat and a hazy insect-ridden ten o'clock. The trees across the courtyard were bare. A solitary five-lobed leaf at the end of a branch resembled a hand thrust out of a window to test for rain.

Zébun sighed. 'I hope Alice does come. I would like to send her to the mosque for news of Maulana Hafeez.'

The sound of the doorbell had diverted the child's attention from the game. Now he lowered his head again and, with a suspicious finger, made certain that his opponent had pushed the counters along the board by the correct number of squares. The bell sounded again. Yusuf Rao's youngest daughter was sitting halfway up the staircase, touching up with colouring pencils the faded cover of a story book. The other children were in one of the bedrooms, with the curtains drawn, shaking awake the fireflies they had captured and imprisoned inside bottles to make lanterns two evenings ago. They, too, ignored the bell. The lawyer's eldest daughter lifted the lid off the yoghurt pan and smiled: the milk had taken – it rarely did during the rainy season. The girl was not allowed to answer the door. Once after a visit from a girl she had met at the Qur'anic lessons, she was severely beaten by her mother: 'So you think you're old enough to make friends? Who gave you permission?' Now she stood in the kitchen, her palms pressed against the clay pot made warm by the overnight activity of the bacteria, and listened to her mother answering the door.

'Who is it?'

'Is Yusuf Rao in, apa-ji?'

'Who is it?' the woman asked, from behind the door.

'The police. The police inspector.'

The woman held her head as one deeply considering. 'No,' she said after a silence 'He's gone to Rawalpindi.'

Through the wooden planks she heard the inspector's sigh; and: 'When is he coming back?'

'I don't know.'

'He didn't say?'

'No.'

The inspector's voice became ingratiating. 'Listen, apa-ji. I just need Yusuf Rao to accompany me to the courthouse for a few minutes and answer a few questions, that's all. You must have heard about the attempt on the General's life. This is all tied up with that. Just a few questions . . .'

'He's away,' Yusuf Rao's wife said, and added, 'brother-ji.'

'I've had orders from Lahore, apa-ji. So you can tell Yusuf Rao that, if he doesn't return from Rawalpindi by this evening, we'll have to force our way into the house.'

The woman stood listening, biting the inside of her lip.

187

The police inspector was saying: 'I respect your purdah, apa-ji. But I have my duty to do. If he doesn't present himself at the courthouse by nightfall I'll have to come into the house.'

Just then the eldest girl came to the kitchen door and looked with frightened eyes at the corner of the courtyard where as a little girl, ten or so years ago, she had watched her mother and father burying books and magazines that would have incriminated her father in the event of a police raid.

Yusuf Rao's wife answered incisively, 'You won't find anyone in here. I've told you already, he's in Rawalpindi.'

At the other side of the door the inspector sighed again, 'I have to go.' He tapped his stick on the wood. 'I have dozens more calls to make before midday.'

The woman secured the door.

As she passed her daughter on the veranda, she said, 'He says he has dozens more calls to make. All this in a town as small and as God-forsaken as this. Imagine what the situation must be like in the cities.'

'I heard everything,' Yusuf Rao said as his wife entered the bedroom. He was dressed for work but had collapsed in a chair. He clasped and unclasped his hands.

'What I want to know,' his wife said, frowning, 'is where that police inspector was last night when they were dragging that poor girl, naked, through the streets. Where were his orders and his duty then?'

Yusuf Rao said distractedly, 'You were against that girl yesterday. Remember?'

'Yes. But I didn't say that a mob should descend on her and drag her by the hair to be left on the doorstep of her parents' house.'

Yusuf Rao breathed noisily through his mouth, from time to time compressing his fleshy lips.

'*I'll have to force my way into the house, apa-ji,*' the woman mimicked. 'He wouldn't dare. If they tried to violate my purdah and enter the house I would scream and shout till the whole street came out in my defence. He'll be sent back to his barracks like the mardood dog that he is. If people can come out against a born-last-Friday Christian harlot then they will also come out to protect a respectable Muslim woman.'

Yusuf Rao looked up sharply. His glance conveyed the tension and anger he was feeling as the rope attached to a mighty sail conveys at a touch the power of the distending wind. 'Typical,' he clenched his fists. 'Typical. The deed's done and, even though we don't approve, let's not waste time thinking about it, *analysing* it. A girl's clothes are torn off in the street, so what? No need to think about how or why it happened. Let's just talk about it as though it's the most natural thing in the world. That's your policy. That's this whole harami country's policy.'

It had happened so quickly. The vehemence shocked them both.

His wife's voice had risen in pitch: 'Some of us don't have time to think. We're too busy trying to get through the day with our hides intact. We don't have time to *analyse*. If you don't agree with what I said then you tell me, Yusuf Rao-*sahib*, what you plan to do when the police inspector comes back with his men tonight. I'm sure you'd be happy to live in gaol for the next six months, eating government-paid chappatis, but I have to think about how I'm going to feed these children of yours.'

She stared at him challengingly.

Their raised voices had attracted the children from the adjoining room. They stood holding the jar full of suffocated fireflies.

'All right, all right.' Yusuf Rao raised his hands. 'But you'll have to think of something, because even if they don't manage to take me away, I won't be able to go to work for the next few months. The office is right in front of the barracks and the courthouse. They've probably already put their own padlock on the door.'

Having spent the preceding eight or so hours in the mosque, Maulana Hafeez returned to his house at noon.

His wife dropped the newspaper and stood up at once to indicate that the distraction had been momentary – her true concern all morning had been Maulana Hafeez.

189

In response to a question about the chill on his lungs Maulana Hafeez shook his head: his health did not require immediate attention. And yet his cheeks were sunken and colourless, the skin waxen; his breathing raspy. He seated himself beside the woman and picked up the newspaper. 'What's in here?'

'You didn't come back for breakfast, Maulana-ji. And you haven't slept.'

'I was praying.'

She leaned towards him, frowning, speaking quietly. 'What happened last night wasn't your fault, Maulana-ji. You mustn't hold yourself responsible. If you hadn't given that sermon then Maulana Dawood would have done so. And soon.'

'I knew that,' Maulana Hafeez said. 'That's why I acted as I did.'

The woman watched the lustreless eyes. There was an odd serenity in the way he spoke – reassurance? delusion?

With the back of his fingers the cleric struck an area near the centre of the newspaper. '*This* kind of thing mustn't be allowed to spread.' He was referring to the phenomenon of mosques being 'conquered' by armed mobs of rival sects. 'Tonight, after Isha, I will visit Maulana Dawood at his mosque.'

The woman nodded, doubtfully. 'They might be hostile, Maulana-ji.' And she pointed at the newspaper, to the item giving news of the latest raided mosque in Lahore.

Maulana Hafeez shook his head. 'But now I have to visit Elizabeth Massih, to see how she is.'

'Is that wise, Maulana-ji?'

Maulana Hafeez inclined his head in a nod, lowering his chin into his collar.

'You shouldn't go there alone, Maulana-ji. Perhaps . . . perhaps I should come with you.'

The cleric considered, stroking his beard, and finally murmured in assent.

While his wife went to collect her cloak Maulana Hafeez gazed vacantly at the newspaper.

Her cloak, the burka – a long cape of white satin draped from a skullcap, with holes at face level – fell in great folds towards the ankles. As she adjusted it, searching for the perforated section, the white moths and butterflies embroidered on the cloth danced in circles around her.

'Hasn't there been any news of her?' Maulana Hafeez asked standing up, when she came back gathering the folds to the front of the chest.

'People have already forgotten about last night, Maulana-ji. The whole town is in turmoil. The deputy commissioner has telephoned back a list of people to be arrested. They say there was an attempt on the General's life two days ago. They've been arresting people since dawn. They shot one man in the shoulder as he tried to escape through his back window. In some cases they've taken children away to force fathers out of hiding.'

'Someone tried to kill the *General*?' Maulana Hafeez asked, incredulous.

'Two days ago,' the woman answered through the holes arranged in a honeycomb pattern before her face. 'The curfew in the big cities which I told you about last night is due to that.'

Maulana Hafeez asked, 'And over the telephone, did the inspector tell the deputy commissioner anything about last night?'

A gentle breeze blew from the west. There was a smell in the air, of sweet pulp rotting.

'I don't know, Maulana-ji.'

The waters were at their yearly highest, the rivers tightening their grip on the town. The narrow lanes of the lower side would soon be under water. The couple would have great difficulty in reaching the Christian neighbourhood.

Maulana Hafeez's wife, walking three paces behind him, asked, 'How do you greet a Christian, Maulana-ji? Can we say *salam-a-lekum*, or is that used just with Muslims?'

Now fully swaddled in cloud, the sun had offered a reluctant profile about an hour ago. Kites and buzzards were wheeling and soaring in the sky.

Maulana Hafeez half turned towards his wife. Nearby a hen papiha peeped. The cleric summoned his remaining strength and tried to think.

*The End*

—

# GLOSSARY OF URDU WORDS

*Aambi*   Unripe mango

*Ahmadiya*   The Ahmadiya movement was founded in 1889 in Northern India by Mirza Gulam Ahmed who proclaimed that he was the Promised Reformer whose advent was awaited by the adherents of Islam. This claim is contested throughout the Islamic world and the Ahmadiyas are denounced as blasphemers. There are, nevertheless, ten million Ahmadiya Muslims living in 120 countries around the world

*Apa*   Form of address of older female

*Asar*   Third prayer of the day

*Baba*   Form of address for old man

*Banéra*   Short wall or filigreed fence used to mark boundaries on flat roof

*Bérry*   Large thorny tree bearing edible berry-like fruit; of jejube family

*Bésan*   Gram flour

*Bhoot*   Ghoul

*Bote*   Fledgling

*Burka*   Cloak

*Chacha-zad*   Cousin

*Chappati*   A flat bread

*Chaval*   Rice

*Chodhi*   Untouchable

*Daig*   Cauldron

*Dhi*   Daughter

*Dhrake*   Tree of Margosa family

*Djinn*   Spirit of supernatural power able to appear in human and animal forms

*Eid*   Festival celebrating the end of the month of Ramadan

*Fakir*   Ascetic/mendicant

*Falsé*   Kind of berry

*Ghat*   Approach to a river

*Goonda*   Henchman

*Gora*   White man

*Gul-é-lala*   Tulip-like tropical plant (*gul*, flower; *lala*, red)

*Harami*   Bastard

*Hira mundi*   The district of prostitutes

*Isha*   Last prayer of the day

*Ishq-é-péchan*   Straggly trailing plant bearing pink and red flowers in bunches (*ishq*, a love affair; *péchan*, complex)

*Jand*   Large tree with white flowers

*Janvar*   Animal

*Jinaza-gah*   Place assigned for funeral prayers

*Kulcha*   Unleavened flat bread

*Kurio*   Girls (sing, *kuri*)

*Langra mango*   Superior variety of mango

*Magrib*   Fourth prayer of the day

*Mahfil*   An evening of pleasure

*Mardood*   Corpse (used as swearword)

*Maulana*   Title and form of address for Muslim clerics

*Mazdoor-Kisan party*   Marxist party (*mazdoor*, labourer; *kisan*, farmer)

*Méva*   Sweetmeat

*Mimber*   Pulpit

*Motya*   Jasmine

*Mukaish*   Form of embroidery done with thin strips of silver

*Na-pak*   Unclean

*Neem*   Margosa tree

*Nyka*   Female brothel keeper

*Papiha*   Migratory bird of cuckoo family; in the poetic traditions of the land which is now Pakistan its cries are represented as heralding monsoon. In prose and in everyday life, the bird is referred to as *koyal*

*Pir*   Holy man

*Punjangala*   Bridal ornament covering back of hands

*Putar*   Son

*Sapas-nama*   Framed tribute presented to dignitary

*Shahzadi*   Princess

*Shamiana*   Marquee

*Soor*   Swine

*Spara*   Qur'anic reader

*Sufi*   Mystic

*Sunnat*   Guidelines derived from the Prophet's daily conduct

*Sura*   Section of the Qur'an. (The Qur'an is made up of thirty
books: these books are further divided into sections called
suras.)

*Surkhi*   Lipstick

*Talli*   Tree related to European beech

*Tamasha*   Public show; a rowdy gathering

*Teddy-paisa*   Popular name of the lowest denomination of coin

*Tindé*   Small green vegetable

*Tur*   Vegetable of cucumber family

*Yaar*   Friend

*Yarkan*   Jaundice

*Zuhr*   Third prayer of the day

Also by Nadeem Aslam

**ff**

# The Blind Man's Garden

Shortlisted for the DSC Prize for South Asian Literature, 2014

Jeo and Mikal are foster-brothers in a small city in Pakistan. Jeo is a medical student who has been married for a year and Mikal is a drifter, in love with a woman he can't have.

After 9/11 as the conflict intensifies in Afghanistan, Jeo decides to secretly enter the country to help care for the wounded, and Mikal goes with him. But can their good intentions keep them out of harm's way?

Left behind is their family, and at its heart their blind father who is haunted by the death of his wife and the mistakes he has made in his life. *The Blind Man's Garden* is an evocative and powerful portrait of ordinary people torn apart by war.

'Extraordinary . . . Once or twice a year a book stuns me. *The Blind Man's Garden* has done just that.' *Independent on Sunday*

'A gripping work that goes to the heart of Muslim fanaticism and Pentagon intransigence alike. Aslam is a wonderful talent and we are lucky to have him.' *Sunday Telegraph*

'[Aslam is] an exceptionally gifted writer . . . *The Blind Man's Garden* is . . . a gripping and moving piece of storytelling that gets the calamitous first act in the "War on Terror" on to the page with grace, intelligence and rare authenticity.' *Guardian*

**ff**

## The Wasted Vigil

Marcus Caldwell, an English widower and Muslim convert, lives in an old perfume factory in the shadow of the Tora Bora mountains in Afghanistan. Lara, a Russian woman, arrives at his home one day in search of her brother, a Soviet soldier who disappeared in the area many years previously, and who may have known Marcus's daughter. In the days that follow, further people arrive there, each seeking someone or something. The stories and histories that unfold, interweaving and overlapping, span nearly a quarter of a century and tell of the terrible afflictions that have plagued Afghanistan – as well of the love that can blossom during war and conflict.

'Unforgettable . . . Tragic and beautifully written. Aslam is a major writer.' A. S. Byatt

'The richest reading experience I had this year . . . a love letter to Afghanistan and also an elegy for its casualties, human and cultural.' Adam Mars-Jones, *Observer* Books of the Year

'My favourite book of this – or any – year . . . A heartbreaking glimpse into the ravages of history . . . I can't recommend it highly enough.' Tahmima Anam, *New Statesman* Books of the Year

# ff

# Maps for Lost Lovers

Winner of the Kiriyama Prize and the Encore Award, and short-listed for the IMPAC Prize

In an unnamed English town, Jugnu and his lover Chanda have disappeared. Rumours abound in the close-knit Pakistani community and then, on a snow-covered January morning, Chanda's brothers are arrested for murder. Telling the story of the next twelve months, *Maps for Lost Lovers* opens the heart of a family at the crossroads of culture, community, nationality and religion.

'Thoughtful, revealing, lushly written and painful, this timely book deserves the widest audience.' David Mitchell, *Mail on Sunday*, Books of the Year

'One of those rare novels that enters your imagination and stays there. Its power comes from the haunting beauty of the language and from excellent characterisation.' Helen Dunmore, *Daily Telegraph*, Books of the Year

'Aslam's vivid and tender portrait of the strict Islamic mother, isolated by her unassailable belief, has stayed with me; as has his metamorphosis of an English town into a poet's universe of flowers, trees and butterflies.' Alan Hollinghurst, *Guardian* Books of the Year